"Fast-moving, exciting, and loaded with straight-forward answers to tough questions, Forbidden Doors is Bill Myers at his best."

Jon Henderson
Author

The Forbidden Doors Series

FORBIDDEN ● DOORS

the undead

JAMES RIORDAN

Based on the Forbidden Doors series created by Bill Myers

TYNDALE Kids

Tyndale House Publishers, Inc.   Wheaton, Illinois

Published in association with the literary agency of Alive
Communications, Inc., 7680 Goddard Street, Suite 200,
Colorado Springs, CO 80920.

Scripture quotations are taken from the *Holy Bible,* New
Living Translation, copyright © 1996. Used by permission of
Tyndale House Publishers, Inc., Wheaton, Illinois 60189. All
rights reserved.

ISBN 0-8423-5740-8, mass paper

Printed in the United States of America

07 06 05 04
6   5   4   3   2

For my son Jeremiah,
who greatly pleases me.

God has not given us a spirit of fear and timidity, but of power, love, and self-discipline.

2 Timothy 1:7

1

She was seventeen—blonde and beautiful.

At least, she would have been beautiful if her features hadn't been twisted into a mask of terror as she screamed.

She backed up slowly, but there was nowhere to go. She was at the end of a dark alley—a dead end. Her heart beat rapidly, and her eyes were wild as she stared into the darkness. She opened her mouth and screamed again.

Two piercing yellow eyes reflected in the light of a distant streetlamp. Powerful eyes. Eyes that burned with an unearthly gleam. Eyes of hate. Of murder.

The girl stopped abruptly. Backed against the wall, she could go no farther. She pressed against the rough brick, trying to get as flat as possible as the eyes approached. Less than six feet away now, the thing began to move more slowly, as if, now that it knew she was trapped, it enjoyed prolonging her agony. The dim glow of the streetlight held no promise of escape—only one of increasing terror as the evil thing floated into view.

It was hideous.

The girl had been silent for several seconds— either resigned to her fate or too drained by fear to scream anymore—but the screams came alive again when, in the shadowy light before her, that part of the fiend that she dreaded most came into view: two long, glistening, white fangs. . . .

"Cut!"

At the word, yelled from the darkness, Jaimie Baylor relaxed against the stone wall.

"Print that one," the director's voice came again from the darkness. "It's a take."

With that, the alley suddenly came alive. Lights blazed on, crewmen swarmed about, and a dozen voices started talking at once.

Dirk Fallon, the director, could be heard above the others. "That's a wrap, people. Break down. Please don't forget to check your morning call times before you leave. Thank you." Jaimie watched as he walked over to her. Although he wasn't a tall man, Fallon's unfriendly nature was intimidating. She knew what was coming and did her best to meet his stern gaze. "Jaimie? I trust you'll be here on time tomorrow?"

She nodded. "I will."

Fallon stared intently at her, and she tried not to fidget. "No problems then with . . . things that go bump in the night. All right?"

"No problems, Dirk," she said, but he was already walking away. She shook her head. He always did that. It was just one of a dozen rude and obnoxious things the man did on a regular basis.

Almost instantly people surrounded Jaimie. A kind-looking, older man from props collected the purse and shopping bag she had been carrying, while a middle-aged woman with brightly dyed red hair took her cape and jewelry. "Just drop the rest off at the costumes trailer before you leave, hon," the woman told her. "I want to press some of the wrinkles out of this dress before we run it over to makeup to get it bloodied."

"No problem," Jaimie replied, forcing a cheery tone, hoping she didn't sound like someone trying to appear happier than she really was.

"You gonna be OK, kid?" the red-haired woman asked as she folded the cape.

Jaimie smiled at her. "I'm OK, Maureen. Thanks for asking."

Nearby, the actor who portrayed the vampire held his mouth open while a young girl from makeup carefully removed his artificial fangs.

"Better be careful you don't cut yourself there," a man in a bulky sweater said as he walked past the two. Jaimie felt herself relax as she recognized Tim Paxton, the producer of the movie.

"Oh, I'm careful, all right," the makeup girl replied. "These teeth are more expensive than my own!"

Paxton laughed. "Great job today, everyone."

"Producers always say that," the propman joked. "Until you ask for a raise."

Paxton laughed again, and Jaimie smiled as she listened to the banter. The producer had the kind of laugh that made a person feel good.

"Have I ever denied you a raise, Bob?" Paxton asked the propman.

Bob shook his head. "No, Tim, you haven't," he replied. "But then, you've never given me one, either."

They both laughed again, but as Tim walked up to Jaimie, a more serious expression came over his face. "You need an escort back to the hotel? I've got a meeting, but I can get someone."

Jaimie held up her hand. "No, Tim. I'll be fine. I think I was just . . . getting into my part too much the other night."

Tim smiled. "OK. That's good to hear. But let me know if you need anything."

"I will," Jaimie replied.

Tim nodded and moved on, making sure to say hello or to joke a bit with most of the cast and crew before they left the set.

"That Tim Paxton is the nicest guy in the movie industry," Maureen, the red-haired costume lady, said as she watched him disappear into the crowd.

"He sure is." Jaimie nodded. "Not like some others I could mention."

They both cast a glance toward Dirk Fallon, who was busy chewing out his cameraman.

"Yeah," Maureen added. "I'd like to take *him* over to makeup to be bloodied instead of this dress."

Jaimie laughed in spite of herself. "Well, I've got to change. See you at the trailer in five, Maureen."

Maureen nodded, but she didn't glance Jaimie's way. She was still staring at Fallon and shaking her head.

~

Twenty minutes later, Jaimie Baylor walked toward the Golden Krone Hotel, feeling better than she had in nearly a week. It was strange enough being only seventeen and acting in *The Vampire Returns,* a horror movie, but filming in Transylvania put things somewhere out in the zone of weirdness as far as she was concerned.

Everything was geared toward vampires here. Even the hotel. When Bram Stoker wrote his *Dracula* novel a hundred years ago, there wasn't a Golden Krone Hotel in Bistrita, but because he had one in the book they wound up building it decades later. And that wasn't all. Bistrita was full of vampire "landmarks," from the names of the hotels and ruins of nearby castles to the items on the menus in the restaurants. With dishes like "Vampire Steak" and "The Count's Chops," it was no wonder Jaimie had a hard time separating her role in the film from reality.

At least, that's what she told herself tonight as she walked through the dimly lit streets. It was the only explanation that made sense. Sure, since filming began a week ago, she'd twice thought she'd seen a real vampire on the streets at night. But what else could you expect in a place like Bistrita?

She shuddered as she recalled the first "sighting." She'd figured it had to be someone in costume, but the second time . . . the second time she was sure whoever—or *whatever*—it was had been stalking her. It had started with echoing footsteps behind her. Every time she had stepped, someone else had stepped. When she stopped, sure enough, she heard footsteps shuffling to a quick stop behind her. That's when she had turned around.

That had been her mistake. That was when she saw yellow eyes and a long black cloak. And that was when she ran back to the set screaming . . . making a total fool of herself in front of the crew.

She sighed at the memory. Of course, they had all teased her about taking her role too seriously, but that didn't change anything. She was still sure she had seen something. Something not quite human . . .

"Stop it!" Jaimie scolded herself. "Stop thinking about it! It wasn't real." She shook her head, determined to put the whole ridiculous incident out of her mind, when . . .

Step.

A chill swept over her. It was the footsteps. Just like before.

She continued walking, her ears straining to hear every sound around her. Most of the time the steps matched hers . . . but not always.

She sped up her pace—the footsteps tried to keep up. Her breathing increased. Someone *was* stalking her. There was no doubt about it.

For an instant she thought of turning around and looking. But remembering how horrified she had been the last time, she decided against it. She couldn't bear seeing that face peering at her again.

So she began to run.

The sound of her tennis shoes on the cobblestones beat out a rhythm in her mind as she raced down the street. There was no mistaking the sound that followed, heavy boots clacking on those same cobblestones.

She reached the top of a small knoll and began to run down the hill. Fog covered the bottom, a ghostly mist patiently waiting to wrap about her.

The gray-and-beige buildings towered above her head. They were centuries old;

their stained walls created a patchwork from decades of replastering. Above them loomed the moonlit mountains—towering, foreboding.

This was no place to be alone. Not here. Not now.

Jaimie reached the bottom of the hill and entered the fog. The footsteps behind her no longer matched her gait. They were more rapid, trying to catch up . . . to close in.

Already she could feel her legs starting to weaken, her lungs starting to burn for more air. She had to slow down. She couldn't keep up this pace. She had to catch her breath.

But the footsteps behind her continued to gain.

She could not, she would not, slow down.

The street snaked its way back up another hill. The incline increased the strain on Jaimie's tortured lungs. Her legs began to lose feeling, as if they were turning to rubber.

And still she forced herself to continue.

Up ahead, glowing through the fog, she saw the lights of the hotel. If she stayed on the winding street, it would be another two or three blocks. If she cut through the approaching alley, she'd shorten the distance by half.

But the alley was dark.

Wouldn't he most likely attack in the dark? Did it even matter?

She felt her legs start to wobble, and she stumbled. She couldn't go much farther. Her lungs felt like they were about to burst; her heart pounded as if it would explode.

She'd have to chance the alley.

She darted to the left and entered the shadowy passageway. Her mind raced with thoughts, terrible images of throats being ripped open, blood streaming down necks, and piercing yellow eyes.

Jaimie knew such images came more from the skills of modern makeup artists and from seeing too many horror movies than from reality, but at the moment they seemed more like her immediate future than someone's warped fantasy.

She continued gasping for air, unable to get enough. Her legs had lost feeling. She wasn't going to make it.

Her right leg betrayed her. It buckled, and she stumbled and tripped. She started to fall but threw out her hand to catch herself against the wall. She succeeded, but in that moment, leaning against the wall, gasping for breath, she stole a look over her shoulder.

A stupid mistake, she knew it even as she turned her head—but she had to see.

And there, racing toward her in the shadows, was her worst fear.

A vampire.

As it ran toward her, its great black cape billowed out and above like two giant bat wings beating against the night air.

Blind terror forced a scream from Jaimie's burning lungs. She shoved herself away from the wall and started running again. She could see the lighted end of the alley, but she'd never reach it. Her legs no longer worked.

They gave way, and she fell . . . tumbling, sliding. Rolling onto her back, she looked up at the approaching figure and screamed again.

∼

Rebecca Williams walked down the steps of the Golden Krone Hotel, accompanied by Ryan Riordan, her boyfriend. At least, that's what everyone they knew considered him. But neither Rebecca nor Ryan felt totally comfortable with the whole boyfriend-girlfriend label. Maybe it was the sexual pressure such a relationship could put on them. Becka wasn't sure. But she was sure of one thing: There was no one she wanted to hang out with more than Ryan, and for some reason she couldn't figure out, he seemed to feel the same way about her.

She often marveled at how good-looking he was. With his thick black hair and bright blue eyes, he could speed up any girl's heartbeat. And when he flashed that amazing grin of his, any red-blooded female was liable to go into cardiac arrest. Even here, thousands of miles from home, girls stopped and stared at him as he went by. But it wasn't his looks that got to Becka. What really touched her were his feelings for her. Her. Plain old Rebecca Williams, who was too tall and had way-too-thin, mousy brown hair. What did he see in her, anyway?

Her best friend, Julie, had laughed when Becka asked her that question. "He sees *you*, silly. The kind of person you are inside."

Becka didn't feel that she was all that great a person inside, either. But she was grateful for whatever it was Ryan saw in her.

"It's kind of pretty here," Ryan said, pulling Becka from her thoughts. "I mean, in a weird sort of way."

Becka nodded. "It's like someplace in a dream."

It was true. In fact, so far the whole trip seemed like a dream. Maybe it was because Becka never thought about going to Transylvania. To be honest, until a few days ago, she hadn't even been sure the place existed outside of movies and horror novels.

But here they were, less than a week after Z's mysterious e-mail.

Things were like that with Z. Ever since he'd started communicating with Rebecca and her younger brother, Scott, on the Internet. All they knew about him was his screen name. They'd never been able to find out his real name, much less anything about him. But, for whatever reason, he had singled out the two of them. For the last year or so, he'd been carefully guiding and directing them in their faith, equipping them with information and truths from the Bible as they helped people who were caught up in the occult. First there had been that group in their own town that had been playing with Ouija boards, then the hypnosis that had almost destroyed Becka, the satanist group that had tried to curse Becka—and on it had gone, from counterfeit hauntings to demons disguised as angels, to UFOs, to voodoo in Louisiana.

So when Z had sent them tickets to Transylvania last week and asked them to help a young actress there, they'd started packing. Of course, Mom came along, too. Rebecca and Scott's father had disappeared in a plane crash in the Brazilian jungle, and the tragedy had brought the three remaining family members even closer. But for some reason, Z had thought Ryan would be better suited for this trip than Scott. And since Z had sent only three tickets and since he'd never been wrong before, Mom agreed that Scott should stay behind with their aunt back in California.

Becka couldn't be happier. Of course, she loved her little brother, but sometimes his sense of humor really got on her nerves. Besides, what could be more romantic than going off to some faraway country with her heartbreaker boyfriend!

OK, so maybe they weren't officially boyfriend and girlfriend, and maybe it was a pretty weird country, and maybe her mom was tagging along a little too much, but still—

This time Becka's thoughts were interrupted by a man in a bulky blue sweater coming out of the hotel. "Excuse me," he called to them, "are you the people who just arrived from America? I'm Tim Paxton, the producer of the film."

"Hello, Mr. Paxton." Ryan and Becka extended their hands.

The producer continued. "There was a message for me at the desk. You want to see Jaimie Baylor?"

"Yes," Ryan said. "We were wondering where to find her, and the hotel clerk said you would be the best person to ask, Mr. Paxton."

"Please, call me Tim," he said, flashing a smile that made Becka immediately feel at ease. "I'm afraid we're all a bit hard to reach at the moment. Just finished shooting for the day, and everyone's probably gone to eat somewhere. But, if you'd like, I'll take you over to the set. Jaimie was still there when I left a little while ago."

"That would be great," Becka replied. She had never seen a movie set. This would be fun.

Tim led them down the old cobblestone road at a brisk pace. "Sorry to hurry you, but it's been a long day, and I'm sure the gang won't hang around long. You guys friends of Jaimie's from Chicago?"

"Uh, well no, not exactly," Becka said, wondering what the producer would say once he found out they had never even met her. But she didn't have time to worry for long. An ear-piercing scream sliced the air, and they spun around.

"What was that?" Becka cried.

"It came from there!" Ryan said, pointing to a dark alley just behind them. He and Tim Paxton ran toward the alley, with Becka close behind—but as soon as she reached the edge of the alley, she stopped cold, frozen by what she saw.

Thirty feet away, a young blonde girl was lying on the street, holding her hands over her face, screaming. And leaning over her was a large figure in a black cape.

Instantly, Tim and Ryan charged down the alley.

At first the creature hesitated, as if it intended to attack the two men. Then he turned with a great flurry of his cape and sped off, quickly disappearing into the night.

2

It was some time
before Jaimie calmed down. In fact, they had
been back in her hotel room for almost an
hour before she fully realized that Becka and
Ryan had come to Transylvania specifically to
see her.

"To see me?" she asked, her hazel green
eyes wide as she looked at Ryan. "You came
all the way here to see me?"

"I guess *we* forgot to tell you in all the excitement," Becka said, careful to emphasize the *we*. It was all too obvious that Jaimie had noticed Ryan's good looks. "But *we* came here to help you."

Jaimie looked at her in surprise. "Help me? How?"

"Do you have a computer?" Ryan asked.

Jaimie nodded. "Sure. My laptop's over there by the phone. Only really talk to a couple of people and—"

"Does one of them call himself 'Z'?" Becka asked.

"Z? Well, yeah," Jaimie said. "Do you know him?"

"In a way," Ryan answered. "Becka and her brother talk to him on the Net all the time."

"He's the one who sent us," Becka added. "He bought us the tickets and told us you needed some help."

Jaimie looked bewildered. "He did?"

Becka and Ryan nodded.

Jaimie thought for a moment. "You know, I told him all about the film and my fears and everything. There wasn't anyone here I could confide in, so I talked to him. I figured, since he didn't really know me, it couldn't hurt. But . . ." She frowned.

"But what?" Ryan asked.

"Well, I used the code name Lucy Westenra."

"Who?" Becka asked.

"You know, the girl who was attacked in the original *Dracula* novel. I used her name. I wonder how this Z fellow knew it was me."

"He's pretty clever," Becka said.

"Maybe it's because this is the only movie on vampires being made here," Ryan said. "And since you're the only girl starring in it . . ."

"I guess that could tip a person off." Jaimie closed her eyes, and a quiet sob escaped her.

"Hey, you OK?" Ryan asked.

She nodded and tried unsuccessfully to fight back tears. "I just can't believe what's happening," she said in a choked voice.

"Don't cry," Ryan said, moving in to comfort her. "You're making me feel terrible."

"I'm sorry," Jaimie said, looking up at him, "but if it wasn't for you and Tim . . . I don't know."

Becka watched Jaimie. For some reason, she didn't entirely believe the girl's tears. Of course, Jaimie had every right to be frightened, but Becka couldn't quite fight off the feeling that this beautiful blonde movie star was using the moment to play up to Ryan. She could be wrong, but still . . .

Maybe it was time to address the vampire

business. To put what was happening in the light of the truth. "Jaimie—" she cleared her throat—"I don't know why this is happening or who is doing this, but we can't let it cloud our thinking."

Jaimie glanced at her quizzically.

Becka continued. "Vampires aren't real. I mean, we all know that. Someone was just trying to scare you, that's all."

"Easy, Beck," Ryan cautioned. "This poor girl's been through a horrible experience."

Becka blinked in surprise. Why were guys always such suckers for girls in tears?

Jaimie just looked up at him, blinking back the tears as she reached out and patted his hand. "Thanks, Ryan."

He nodded, then looked back at Becka. "I don't think Jaimie needs someone putting her through a hard-boiled reality check just yet, do you?"

The words hit Becka like a slap in the face. She blinked again. Maybe she'd been wrong. It was obvious Jaimie was still struggling with what had happened. And you really couldn't blame her for turning to someone like Ryan for comfort.

Maybe he was right; maybe she shouldn't have brought it up so soon. "I'm sorry," she said softly. "I didn't mean . . ." She let the words trail off.

"It's OK," Jaimie replied. "It's just that people on the set have been making fun of me ever since the last time I saw it."

Ryan looked at her, surprised. "This has happened before?"

Jaimie nodded and told them about her previous encounter with the vampire—the footsteps, the billowing black cape, the yellow glowing eyes, and her panicked race to the film set only to be met with the cast and crew's laughter and joking.

"Well, at least no one will be telling me I imagined this one," she said. "No one's going to tell me I'm taking my role too seriously now. Not when other people have seen him, too."

Ryan agreed.

"Why would someone want to scare you like that?" Becka asked.

"Scare me?" Jaimie's voice rose. "The vampire was trying to *kill* me."

"Jaimie," Becka remained quietly firm, "there simply isn't such a thing as a vampire. I'm sure he looked very frightening, but that was just some guy trying to scare you."

Jaimie stared hard at Becka. Then she reached up and pulled the collar of her turtleneck sweater down a bit. "If he was just trying to scare me, why did he do this?"

Becka caught her breath.

Two long scratches ran down Jaimie's neck. They were not bites really—they were more the kind of mark that would be made if two huge fangs had suddenly pulled away before they could complete the kill.

The next day, Ryan, Becka, and Mrs. Williams all went down to watch the filming. Though Jaimie was still unknown as an actress and though *The Vampire Returns* was a fairly low-budget movie, they were all excited about visiting the set.

"Are you sure we won't be in the way?" Mom asked as they left the hotel.

"We'll be OK," Ryan answered. "Besides, Jaimie said she'd feel better if we were there."

"Nobody else connected with the film is even close to her age," Becka explained, "and she's still pretty shaky. She feels like she can relate to us best."

"So what do you kids think really happened to this girl?" Mom asked as they walked down the alley.

"I've read of cases where deranged people actually believed they were vampires," Becka said.

"Really?" Mom asked.

"Even enough to bite people in the neck?" Ryan inquired doubtfully.

"Even enough to kill them and drink their blood," Becka replied. "There was this guy in Germany who was convinced he had a blood disease that required him to drink human blood every so often to stay alive."

"That's a cheery thought," Mom said.

Ryan added, "Well, if some guy's actually attacking her, trying to bite her neck, then it really doesn't matter whether he's a real vampire or not. He's just as dangerous."

"Well, in one sense, yes," Becka agreed, "but in another sense, it matters a lot."

"Why's that?" Ryan asked.

Becka met his look. "A real vampire would be a lot more dangerous to catch."

When they arrived at the set, Jaimie and another actor were preparing to film a scene. Becka was surprised at how much equipment and how many crew members were involved. Even though it was the middle of the day, several big lights glowed from large stands. High overhead and spanning across two rooftops, a gigantic canvas made of some sort of reflective material overlooked the set.

"I thought this was supposed to be a small production," Ryan said.

"Think what a big production must be," Becka answered.

All around people scurried about, doing their jobs to set up the scene. Men were lay-

ing some sort of track in front of a large cart
that held the camera. Several stagehands
were positioning huge blocks to look like a
castle wall, the lighting crew was aiming the
lights, prop people were placing flags,
torches, and weapons at various places on
the wall, and the hair and makeup folks were
putting the finishing touches on the actors.

Suddenly, the assistant director's voice bel-
lowed, "We're ready, people. Settle in,
please. Nice and quiet."

Instantly, all action stopped. No one
moved. No one spoke.

Ryan, Becka, and Mom stood on a small
knoll overlooking the scene. From this location they could see everything.

Jaimie and an older man stood on the
makeshift castle wall, waiting to begin.

The director rose from his canvas chair
and walked over to the cameraman. He
looked briefly through the lens to confirm
the shot and then nodded back to the assistant director.

"Stand by!" the assistant director called.
"Roll sound."

"Speed," a man sitting at a tape recorder
responded.

"Camera?" the assistant director asked.

"Rolling," the cameraman said.

"Mark it."

A young man with a clapboard stepped between the camera and the actors. "Scene 35, take one." he snapped the board shut and stepped out of the way.

"And . . . action!" the director called.

Jaimie and the older man began to walk—Jaimie up on the wall, the man on the castle walkway a few feet below. The camera followed them on the tracks very low to the ground and shooting up so that it looked like they were very high, when in reality they were only a few feet off the ground.

"I tell you, I'm all right, Robert," Jaimie shouted back to the actor as she threaded her way slowly along the top of the wall. "There's no need for you to keep me inside at night anymore."

The man shook his head. He spoke in a thick German accent and crossed his arms when he spoke. "You are not all right, I tell you. You have been bitten by one of the lords of the night, and if you even so much as smell the night air, your very blood will cry out to him. And he will find you and take you and make you his slave for all eternity. Is that what you want?"

From the knoll, Becka and Ryan exchanged glances. The scene was quite convincing.

On the set, Jaimie stared at the man for a

long moment while the camera slowly and silently dollied in for a closer shot. "Of course not," she said. "But am I to be a prisoner in this house every night?"

The man nodded firmly. "Yes, until we catch the vampire."

With his thick accent, he pronounced *vampire* as if it were spelled *vampeer*. A long moment of silence passed, during which Jaimie turned and took a few steps away from the man. Then she began to wobble, as if losing her balance on the high wall.

"Stop!" the older man shouted. "Don't move or you might fall. Let me come to you."

He carefully walked toward her.

Jaimie regained her balance and turned back to him to shout, "What if you never catch him?"

"Cut!" The director yelled and then walked over to Jaimie. "Jaimie, Jaimie, Jaimie. Sweetheart, you've got to take more steps away from him before delivering that line. It looks too forced this way. Walk as if you're still planning on escaping down the roof, and then spin around and say it to him. All right?"

Jaimie nodded, and the director was starting to walk back when Maureen, the wardrobe lady, came up to him and said something.

Clearly frustrated, the director shouted, "Break! Five minutes while Maureen does the work she should have done before we started!"

Instantly, the set filled with noise and commotion. Maureen ran over to Steve Delton, the actor playing Van Helsing, and helped take off his waistcoat. Quickly and efficiently, she began stitching a button that had come loose.

Jaimie looked up and spotted Ryan and Becka. "Hi, guys!" she shouted. "I'll be there in a minute, just as soon as I get my hair checked."

Suddenly, the director's voice sounded through his megaphone. "Jaimie, stay here. If you go climbing up that hill, your hair will need to be done again. Your friends can come down here to talk to you."

Becka was embarrassed, but Jaimie's friendly wave encouraged her to come down and talk to her.

"Mom," Becka said, turning to speak to her mother, "are you coming with—" but she stopped.

Her mother was several yards away, talking with a rugged-looking man carrying a camera and cassette recorder.

"Mom," she called, "are you coming?"

"No, I'm fine here, dear," she said. "Tell Jaimie hi for me."

The rugged man leaned toward Mom, saying something to her. She laughed and tossed her hair to the side—a clear sign that she was nervous.

"Who's that guy?" Becka asked as she and Ryan descended the hill.

Ryan shrugged. "Who knows? He seems to like your mother, though."

"That's what I mean."

"It's OK," Ryan said as he picked up his pace to head down the hill. "I'm sure she can take care of herself. Come on, let's hurry."

"Yeah," Becka said. She was still concerned, but not so much over Mom as over the way Ryan was suddenly racing ahead of her to see Jaimie. Was it her imagination, or did he seem just a bit too eager? Actually, he seemed a *lot* too eager. By the time Becka finally caught up to him, Jaimie was already introducing him to her friends on the set.

"You've been holding out on us, Jaimie," Maureen chuckled as Becka approached. "Keeping a cute guy like this stashed away."

Everybody laughed, including Ryan.

What's he *laughing about?* Becka wondered as she carefully positioned herself between Jaimie and Ryan.

"Oh, and this is Becka," Jaimie added. Unfortunately, no one paid much attention as they spotted Dirk Fallon, the director, heading in their direction. Suddenly, they all made themselves scarce.

As Fallon approached, Becka couldn't help noticing that the guy had a major attitude. "Who does he think he is?" she whispered to Jaimie.

Jaimie shushed her. "He's the director."

"I know," Becka whispered back. "But why does he have to act so—"

"Are we ready to go again, Jaimie?" Fallon interrupted as he approached. Becka could see that the man's very presence made Jaimie nervous.

"Yes, Dirk, I'm ready," Jaimie said. "Oh, by the way, these are my friends from—"

"I'll meet them later, dear," he said, cutting her off. "We've got a picture to make." Then, without waiting for a response, he spun around and nodded to the assistant director.

"Places, everyone," the assistant director shouted. "We're ready."

The activity on the set accelerated dramatically as the actors and the crew resumed their positions for filming.

"Talk to you later," Jaimie whispered to Ryan. She gave Becka a friendly nod and hurried to her place.

Ryan motioned over his shoulder toward the director as he and Becka headed back up to the top of the knoll. "That guy's a real jerk."

Becka nodded. "I don't think I like film people."

"Well, Jaimie's real nice."

Becka met his gaze. "Is she?"

"Sure . . . I mean, well, yeah." He eyed her, confused. "What do you mean?"

"Nothing, I guess. She just seems kind of phony, if you ask me."

Ryan studied her for a minute. "Beck, you don't think you're, maybe, a little jealous, do you?"

"Jealous!" Becka said the word so loudly that the nearest crew members looked up at them.

"Easy! You'll get us tossed out of here."

She lowered her voice. "What do you mean, I'm jealous?"

Ryan shrugged. "I just meant that since she's a star and everything—"

"She's not a star. This is only her second film, and nobody saw the first one."

"I know, I know, but she does get treated pretty special."

"So?"

"So, maybe all the attention she gets is bothering you a little."

They had reached the top of the hill, and Becka stared at him dully. "Yeah, I guess it does. I guess all the attention she gets does bother me."

Ryan nodded. "You see. But that's just how these people are. Everybody makes a big deal of the star."

Becka stared at him. "I guess they do," she said in cool tones. He didn't respond, didn't even seem to notice her displeasure. Without another word, she turned and started toward her mother. She could feel Ryan's eyes on her, and she could tell he still didn't get it.

Guys . . . they could be so clueless sometimes.

Mom and the rugged man were still talking, and as Becka approached, they started to laugh. "What's so funny?" she asked.

"Oh, nothing," Mom said. "John was just telling me what a hard time he's had adjusting to the customs here in Transylvania. He's a reporter from New York."

"Hi, Becka," the man said. "I'm John Barberini. With *Preview* magazine."

"Hi," Becka said, doing her best to sound pleasant, though she didn't much like him. "So, you're doing a story on the film?"

"I sure am. And it looks like I'm in luck. This vampire business will make for great copy."

"You don't believe it, do you?" Becka asked.

"I didn't say I believed it, just that it makes for a great story."

"John has offered to show us some good places to shop," Mom said. "You can bring Ryan."

"Who wants to?" Becka muttered under her breath, then added out loud, "Ryan and I, we sort of made plans to hang out with Jaimie. Maybe we can do it anoth—"

"Guess we'll have to settle for a duet then," John said, turning to Mom and smiling just a little too broadly.

To Becka's surprise, Mom smiled back.

"Becka . . ." It was Ryan coming up the hill. "Becka, can I talk to you?"

Becka turned to him, but before she could speak, the assistant director shouted through his megaphone, "Quiet, please! Stand by. Roll sound."

"Speed," came the response.

"Camera?"

"Rolling."

"Marker."

"Scene 35, take two!"

"And . . . action!" Dirk Fallon shouted.

Once again, Steve Delton, the actor playing Van Helsing, delivered his line. "Yes, until we catch the *vampeer.*"

Only this time Jaimie took several steps along the wall before turning around and saying, "What if you never catch him?"

Van Helsing walked toward her. "We will catch him, my dear. I promise you. Please, come down from there. You need your rest. And here, I've brought something for you."

He took out of his pocket a golden chain, from which dangled a large and ornate cross. "Wear this at all times. It is your only protection."

She knelt down so he could reach up and put the necklace over her head.

But as soon as the crucifix touched her skin, Jaimie shrieked in pain. Her knees buckled, her body crumpled, and she half rolled, half fell off the small wall onto the ground.

Ryan and Becka thought it was all part of the script until Fallon shouted, "Cut! Cut! What happened? Is she all right?"

Delton stood helplessly over Jaimie's still form. It was clear from his expression that he was no longer playing a role. "I don't know," he said as crew members quickly circled around Jaimie. "She fainted. Quick, somebody get a doctor. Somebody get a doctor!"

3

"It looks like an acid burn to me," the crotchety old doctor said as he carefully examined Jaimie's neck. She lay on the sofa inside her dressing-room trailer. An angry red mark now covered the red scratch she'd had from before.

"Acid?" Tim Paxton exclaimed. "How can that be? Where's that cross?"

Tim was one of several onlookers inside

Jaimie's trailer, a group that also included Ryan and Becka. Very carefully, a propman handed Tim Paxton the cross. The producer looked at it closely for a long moment and then pushed up the sleeve of his jacket.

Everyone waited in expectation as he pressed the cross against his own skin.

But nothing happened. No burn, no pain. Nothing.

Tim sighed. He looked back to the red mark on Jaimie's neck and shook his head. "I'm sorry, Jaimie. I don't know what's going on, but I promise you, we'll get to the bottom of this."

Jaimie did her best to put on a brave smile.

A light flashed suddenly, and Becka turned to see John Barberini lowering his camera.

"Who let him in here?" Tim Paxton shouted.

"Take it easy. I'm going, I'm going," Barberini said as he left the trailer.

"You'd better not use that shot!" Tim called after him. Then, looking to the group inside, he added, "I think it might be good if we all leave. Jaimie needs some rest."

The crowd agreed and started to move out.

"We'd better get back to the hotel," Becka whispered to Ryan. "I think it's time we contacted Z."

Ryan nodded, but before they got to the

door, Jaimie called out, "Ryan, could you please stay for a while? I don't want to be alone."

Ryan looked to Becka. "Maybe I should stick around. I mean, if you don't mind."

"It would sure be helpful for us," Tim said from behind them. "You always seem to pick up her spirits a little."

Ryan nodded but continued to wait for Becka's response.

Becka bit the inside of her lip. What was wrong with him? Couldn't he see what Jaimie was pulling? But before she could answer, Jaimie interrupted.

"Say, Tim? Remember how we talked about needing someone to go over my lines with me?"

Tim nodded. "A dialogue coach, of course. But I haven't found anyone who—"

"What about Ryan?" she asked. "Couldn't we hire him?"

Becka's eyes darted to Tim.

"Well, yeah," he said, "I guess we could. If he wanted to do something like that. I mean, I can't pay much, but if he wants the job—"

"Are you kidding?" Ryan exclaimed. "A job with a movie? I'd love it!"

Tim chuckled and held out his hand. "Then it looks like we've got ourselves a deal."

An excited Ryan shook the producer's hand.

"Just find out when Jaimie's breaks are each day and read through the upcoming scenes with her," Tim said. "And I'll go ahead and add you to the payroll. How does seventy-five a day sound?"

"Seventy-five . . . dollars?" Ryan croaked.

Tim smiled. "And all the food you can eat."

Ryan spun around to Becka, not believing his good luck. "Wow! I'm in showbiz!"

Becka could only stare.

Spotting the look of concern on her face, he asked, "Are you all right? I mean, this is cool with you, right?"

Part of Becka wanted to shout at him or slug him. How could he be so insensitive? so dense? But the other part, the "mature adult" part, knew that this was a great opportunity for him. Besides, it wasn't like they were married or anything.

So, before she could stop herself, Becka said, "Do what you want, Ryan. I mean, if that's what you want, then go for it."

"Are you sure?" he asked.

She just looked at him. He was so thoughtful and sensitive . . . and clueless.

"Sure." She shrugged. "Whatever."

Suddenly Dirk Fallon poked his head into the trailer. "So what's the story?"

Tim turned to the doctor. The old man had just finished treating Jaimie's neck with an ointment and answered, "Nothing serious. Just a minor acid burn."

"Acid burn?" Fallon's voice sounded both shocked and skeptical.

The doctor nodded. "I put some salve on it. Let her rest for a while, and she'll be fine."

"How long of a while?" Fallon asked. "We're trying to make a movie here, you know."

"A few hours at least," the doctor said as he put his things into a leather bag and prepared to leave the trailer.

"A few hours?" Fallon turned to his producer, incredulous. "We've lost an hour and a half here already, Tim. We're falling way behind schedule."

"Calm down, Dirk."

"Calm down? Calm down?" the director's voice was rising.

"The girl's had a rough time," Tim said.

Fallon shook his head. "Yeah, well, just don't get upset when we run over schedule and out of money."

Tim was not giving any ground. "If we run out of money—and I do mean *if*—as the producer *I'll* be the one who has to deal with getting more. Correct?"

By way of an answer, Fallon turned from

the trailer door, hoisted his megaphone, and shouted, "Two-hour break for principal cast. Crew, set up for the next shot."

Meanwhile, Becka had stepped from the trailer and was angrily making her way toward the hotel.

"Rebecca?" It was Tim Paxton calling. "Becka?"

She slowed her pace as he joined her. "Say, I hope you don't mind about me hiring Ryan."

"Why would I mind?" she lied.

"It's just that he seems to be a real comfort to Jaimie, and I think she needs all the help she can get right now."

"Why are you telling me?" she asked. "Ryan can do what he wants. It's not like he's my boyfriend or anything." As soon as the words came out, she regretted them. Sure, she and Ryan tried not to use the terms *boyfriend* and *girlfriend,* but there had always been an understanding between them. Or at least there had been until Jaimie came into the picture.

"Really?" Tim studied her face curiously. "I just sort of assumed . . . well, that's great then, for everyone, I mean." Tim checked his watch. "Well, I'd better go. Gotta get back in there and fight with the director. We'll see you a little later."

Becka forced a smile as he turned and walked away. She headed for the hotel, determined not to focus on the fact that she'd more than likely made a bad situation even worse.

~

Back at the hotel, Rebecca was surprised to see John Barberini, the reporter, in the lobby. "Hi there," he said. "Tell your mother I'm here, will you? I'm ready to do some serious shopping."

Becka nodded. "All right."

"Sure you don't want to join us?"

She shook her head. "No, I've got . . . something I have to do." Becka started to leave but then felt Barberini's strong hand on her shoulder.

"So what do you think about that crucifix business? Is that girl turning into a vampire or what?"

Becka stared at him. "What do you mean?"

"Well, I may not be up on my vampire lore, but when somebody's been bitten by a vampire and then her skin gets burned by the touch of a crucifix . . . sounds to me like she's turning."

"Turning?"

"Yeah, you know. That's how it works, right? If somebody gets bitten by a vampire, that person turns into one, too."

Suddenly an image of Jaimie sinking her own fangs into Ryan's neck flashed into Becka's mind. She swallowed and answered coolly, "I don't believe in such things." She turned away, then called back over her shoulder, "I've got to go. I'll tell Mom you're here."

Barberini nodded and smiled a crude sort of smile, which made her like him even less. She crossed to the elevator, went inside, and pressed the button. When the door closed, she leaned against the back wall for support. Everything seemed to swirl so fast now. Ever since she'd arrived here, she'd felt like she was in some sort of crazy dream. And now the dream seemed to be turning into a nightmare.

"Mom," she said as she entered their hotel suite, "that creepy reporter guy's waiting downstairs for you."

Mom looked up from applying her makeup in front of the dresser mirror. "What's bothering you?"

Becka shrugged. "Nothing. I just think that guy is a total jerk."

"You don't even know him," Mom said, her tone a little more firm than before.

"You should've seen him snapping pictures of the doctor examining Jaimie in her trailer."

"Honey, that's his job."

"I just get the feeling he's glad that all this is happening, that's all."

Mom leaned into the mirror for one last check and then stood up. "I doubt he's glad, sweetheart. But it is his job to cover what's happening here."

Becka watched her mother put the finishing touches to her hair. Finally she said what had been rattling in the back of her head. "John's not a Christian, is he?"

Mom paused, then turned to face her. "No, Rebecca, I don't think he is."

"You always say I shouldn't date a non-Christian, so what are you—"

"Rebecca, he just offered to help me do a little shopping."

"Yeah, but—"

"Honey, I know this is hard for you, but you have to trust me. I'm not dating John. We're just going shopping. Now, I have to go. We'll talk later, honey. All right?"

Becka took a deep breath and slowly let it out. Her mom was trying her best to be open and fair. Maybe she should do likewise. "All right," Becka said. "I'll see you when you get back."

Mom smiled. As she picked up her purse and crossed for the door, she gave Becka a gentle peck on the cheek. "Bye, honey." She opened the door, then turned back one last time. "And don't worry so. Everything will be just fine."

Becka nodded and cranked up another smile before Mom turned and headed out the door.

Later, as she unpacked the laptop and plugged in the power adapter, Becka felt bad about quizzing Mom. After all, it was just shopping. As a single parent, her mom had been through a lot. Ever since Dad's plane crash, she'd been the one who'd had to hold the family together. And if some guy showed a little interest and offered to be helpful, wasn't she at least entitled to that? Besides, Mom was a big girl. She could take care of herself.

At least, Becka hoped she could.

Carefully, she switched on the laptop, accessed the Internet, and typed in Z's address. She planned to leave a message for him to contact her the next time he was on-line, but she was in luck. He was already there, waiting.

Hello, Rebecca. How do you like Transylvania?

As the words came across the screen, Becka felt better. Hearing from Z usually gave her a sense of peace. In some strange

way it reminded her of when she used to talk
to her father. Maybe it was because he always
seemed to have the answers. Or maybe it was
because she knew he cared.

For the next few minutes Becka typed
away, trying to explain to Z all that had happened since they'd arrived. Every once in a
while he'd ask a question, but mostly he just
listened.

Finally, she'd told him everything . . . well,
just about everything. She'd left out the part
about when she thought Jaimie was putting
the moves on Ryan and how she had been
feeling some major jealousy. After all, that
didn't have anything to do with vampires.

Needless to say, she was more than a little
surprised when Z asked:

How is Ryan doing?

Becka typed one word:

Fine.

She waited, but Z gave no response. That's
what he usually did when he knew there
was more. Finally, almost reluctantly, she
added:

He likes it here.

After a moment, Z asked:

How does he like Jaimie?

Rebecca's mind raced. Had Z known Ryan
would fall for Jaimie? Had he arranged it by
sending Ryan a ticket? Of course, she realized she was being foolish. This was just Z's
way. . . . He always seemed to know what was
happening, whether anybody told him or
not. It was one of the many strange things
about him, and it always made her feel just a
little uneasy. But since he already knew what
was going on, she quit beating around the
bush and typed:

All right, so I'm jealous.

Z typed back:

Remember why you're there.
Jaimie needs your help.

Becka was offended. She'd been *trying* to
help Jaimie—hadn't she been the one to
remind the girl that vampires weren't real?
But it seemed all the pretty actress was inter-
ested in was Ryan. Frustrated, she decided to
change the subject.

What about the vampire?

The response was almost immediate:

There are no such things as vampires.

Becka scowled. Yeah, well, she knew that, but what about everything that had happened? The attacks on Jaimie, the fang marks, the burning cross? *Something* was going on! Before she could type her questions, Z added the following:

I cannot explain all that is happening, but unexplained circumstances don't change truth. And this is the truth: There is no such thing as a vampire.

There he goes again, Becka thought. Sometimes talking to Z could be very confusing. She reached for the keyboard and typed:

So what are we supposed to do?

Z's answer was typical:

Always remember, "God has not given us a spirit of fear." Look past the fear.

Quickly she typed:

How?

Let God's love show through you.

Becka answered immediately:

Yeah, but—

She got no further. Z's message cut her words off:

Must go. Keep me posted. Z

Becka let out a short, frustrated sigh. Part of her felt comforted because Z had confirmed that there were no vampires, but another part was frustrated, angry, and confused.

And right now, that part was winning out.

~

Becka awoke with a start. She had sprawled out on the bed, intending to close her eyes for only a second. A quick glance at the window told her it was already dark outside. She must have slept longer than she'd planned.

As she lay in the darkness, she tried to recall her nightmare. She couldn't remember the details, just the fear and the swirling darkness that twisted throughout the dream like a black, evil snake.

And, of course, the strange tapping sound.

A weird tap-tap-tap had echoed through the dream. It kept coming back, over and over again. She could almost hear it now. In fact . . . she held her breath . . . she *was* hearing it now.

It seemed to come from the window. At first she thought it was a tree branch. Then she remembered they were on the fourth floor.

No trees here went up that high.

Her heart started pounding. She reached over, switched on the light by her bed, and listened.

Tap-tap-tap.

Tap-tap-tap.

She fought the fear that made her want to crawl under the covers and wait for the sound to go away.

Tap-tap-tap.

Tap-tap-tap.

She had to find out what it was.

Tap-tap-tap.

Tap-tap-tap.

Slowly, mustering all the courage she could find, she eased her feet over the side of the bed.

Tap-tap-tap.

Tap-tap-tap.

Carefully, absolutely silent in her stocking feet, she approached the closed curtain.

Tap-tap-tap.

She swallowed hard. The thought of racing out of the room tantalized her, but she knew she'd be wondering about the noise all night. No, it was better to confront the fear now. Besides, didn't this sort of thing always turn out to be something silly?

Tap-tap-tap.

She carefully reached for the curtain. Her mind swam with a thousand thoughts. Where was Mom? It was dark out, and she still wasn't back from shopping. Where was Ryan? How come he hadn't called? Was he still with Jaimie? Jaimie, who might be turning into a vampire. Jaimie, who may be turning Ryan into—

Tap-tap-tap.

Becka took another deep breath. It was nothing. She was sure of it. Just a silly bird or a lost kite or—

Tap-tap-tap.

Tap-tap-tap.

It was time. She jerked open the curtain and went stone cold. Floating in midair and grinning at her grotesquely, the hideous form of a vampire hovered outside the window. His long sharp fangs gleamed like miniature pearl knives.

But it was the yellow eyes that sent the chill through Becka. They held a lifeless evil. A deadness and depravity that spoke of centuries of horror . . . centuries of murder.

His death white hand stretched out, and one long fingernail extended toward the window, rapping against the glass.

Tap-tap-tap.

Tap-tap-tap.

Becka could not breathe. Her eyes were riveted to the creature's yellow gaze, yet somehow she managed to back away.

Tap-tap-tap.

Tap-tap-tap.

And then she turned and ran.

4

*B*y the time she reached the lobby of the hotel, Becka realized there was no place to go. She certainly didn't want to go out into the night with the vampire right outside her window . . . and she sure wasn't going back up to her room.

She could tell the desk clerk to call security, that a vampire was hanging out in front of her window, but somehow she had her doubts that she'd be taken seriously.

She decided to hide out downstairs on the main floor. She had a Diet Coke at the snack bar but didn't eat anything. For some reason she no longer thought "Dracula Burgers" or "Ladyfingers with Onion Rings" were that amusing.

She browsed the newsstand, but the local papers all showed Jaimie's face on the front page. "He's Baaaaack!" one English headline read, leading readers into the story about Jaimie's alley encounter.

Wonderful. Now her archrival was a local celebrity.

She thought of Z's suggestion to love Jaimie. Well, from what she'd just seen, he was wrong about vampires. Maybe he was wrong about this, as well.

At last she came to the lobby. She sat in one of the big leather chairs facing the desk and waited for Mom or Ryan or somebody to come by.

And then she heard it. Giggling. The voice sounded familiar. Almost like Jaimie's. It was followed by a loud guffaw, which sounded like Ryan's laugh.

Slowly, she turned around and peeked over the top of the big leather chair.

It was Ryan, all right—sitting with Jaimie and laughing his fool head off. For one horrible instant, Becka thought they were laughing at her. Then she realized that, even in his worst moments, Ryan was too good a friend for that.

Still, she resented him for not coming back to the hotel with her. If he'd been there with her, maybe the vampire wouldn't have come to her window. And if it had, at least someone else would've seen it. The last thing in the world she wanted to do was look like she was imitating Jaimie. Or, worse yet, look like a fool by insisting that someone was floating outside her window and having everyone say, "But that's impossible. You were on the fourth floor!"

"Becka? What are you doing here?" It was Ryan. He had spotted her spy routine.

"Uh . . . hi, Ryan. . . . Hi, Jaimie." She was flustered but tried her best to hide it. "I just, uh, came down here because . . ."

"Were you looking for me?" Ryan asked.

"No," Becka snapped. "Of course not. I was waiting for Mom. She's out with that reporter guy."

"So why aren't you waiting in your room?" Ryan asked.

There was just no easy way to say it. Finally, Becka blurted, "Because the last time I was there a vampire was tapping on my window."

Ryan looked at her incredulously. "But that's impossible. You're on the fourth floor!"

Even Jaimie looked as if she didn't believe her. "Are you sure, Becka?"

"What's that supposed to mean?"

Jaimie cleared her throat. "Well, it's just that, I mean, so far I'm the only one who's been—"

Becka stood up. "I can't believe you don't believe me. Especially you, Jaimie."

"I'm just suggesting that maybe there's some sort of logical—"

Becka cut her off. "Yeah, right." With that, she stalked toward the elevator. She knew she was overreacting, and by the time she arrived at the elevator doors, she also knew she wasn't about to face her room alone. So she turned around and walked right back to Ryan and Jaimie, who were still watching the performance.

"So," she said, "are you coming up with me to check out the room or what?"

Ryan glanced at Jaimie, then rose to his feet. "Sure. C'mon, Jaimie," he said, "let's go check it out."

Jaimie looked less than excited about the idea but agreed and followed them toward the elevator. As soon as the elevator doors slid shut, Becka felt herself growing tense. Going back to her room to see if a vampire was waiting there to kill her might not be that bright of an idea after all.

Ryan must have been having similar thoughts because he turned to her and asked, "Have you got a crucifix?"

"A crucifix?" Becka said, somewhat confused.

"I've got one," Jaimie said. "It's in my room. Let's go there first."

Two minutes later they were in Jaimie's room, arming themselves with two crucifixes and a small bottle of holy water that a crew member had given the actress.

"Ryan, why are we doing this?" Becka asked as they headed back toward the elevator. "I don't even believe in vampires."

Ryan shrugged. "Do you think you imagined that thing outside your window?"

She shook her head.

"Then we have to fight it, don't we?"

Becka was still confused. "What about spiritual warfare?"

Now Jaimie looked confused. "Spiritual what?"

Ryan's face turned red at Becka's question, and he paused. "She means prayer," he told Jaimie. "And using Scripture."

Jaimie frowned. "Scripture? You mean the Bible?" Her incredulous gaze came back to Becka. "You want to fight a vampire with 'Now I lay me down' and Bible verses?"

Before Becka could respond, Ryan shook his head. "I know I'm still new at this, Beck, but I don't remember anything in the Bible that addresses vampires floating outside your window, do you?"

"Well—"

"Right. So I figure it can't hurt to take this stuff with us just to be safe." He pressed the button.

Becka leaned back against the wall, struggling with the jumble of emotions sweeping over her. Fear. Frustration. Embarrassment. Guilt. Especially guilt. Some spiritual warrior she was. She didn't even know what Scripture to use! And now this business about crosses and holy water. They hardly seemed the right weapons to fight with. And yet . . .

When the elevator doors opened on the fourth floor, Becka felt a cold shiver run through her body. Their suite was just five doors down the hall. Slowly, the three of them made their way toward it. Ryan and Jaimie took the lead, each holding a large crucifix in front of them. Becka followed, carrying the bottle of water.

They arrived at the door. Everything was quiet.

Carefully, Becka inserted her key, but when Ryan reached for the knob she waved for him to stop. "Wait a sec. Let me get ready."

Rebecca's hands trembled as she took the top off the bottle of water. Part of her felt foolish. In all of their encounters with the powers of darkness, they'd never once resorted to things like holy water and cruci-fixes. They'd always attacked things through prayer and by checking out the Bible. To her this other way just seemed like, well, like stu-pid superstitions. Still, Ryan had a point. The Bible didn't say anything about vampires. . . .

She looked up at Ryan, and all three braced themselves.

Finally, she nodded. He threw open the door, and they charged in.

A large form loomed between them and the desk light.

"Get him!" Ryan shouted.

Ryan and Jaimie shoved the crucifixes at the silhouetted figure while Becka threw the water on him.

"Hey! What do you think you're doing?" John Barberini spun around, his hair and shirt dripping.

"Rebecca!" It was Mom, coming out of the other room. "What are you doing?"

A moment of silence passed as Becka strug-gled to find her voice. "We, uh . . . we thought he was a vampire."

~

Once again, Becka explained about the vam-pire outside her window. This so intrigued

John that he pretty much forgave her for the soaking. "I guess I should be glad she didn't drive a stake through my heart instead," he tried to joke.

Everyone chuckled, but Becka's ears burned with embarrassment.

John opened the window and carefully checked out the ledge. When he drew his head back inside, Ryan asked, "Did you see anything?"

John shook his head. "There's no way anybody could rig something to hang out there. Either someone's playing an elaborate joke, or . . ." He hesitated.

"Or?" Jaimie asked.

He spoke slowly and carefully. "Or we've got a real vampire on our hands."

After Mom had called hotel security and after John, Jaimie, and Ryan had finally left for their own rooms, Mom turned to Becka in quiet concern. "Sweetheart, I don't want you to take this the wrong way, but . . ."

"But what, Mom?"

"Well, are you sure none of this has anything to do with John?"

"What?"

"Well, I mean, you seemed sort of sensitive about him taking me shopping."

Becka couldn't believe what she was hearing and let out a groan of exasperation.

"And then you attacked him."

"No, Mother." There was no missing the irritation in her voice.

Mom remained silent as Becka began to pace. "I *saw* what I saw, all right? And if you think I'd attack John because I was jealous or something, well, you're just plain wrong. Besides I didn't *attack* him; I threw water on him. I mean, he's no worse for the wear. . . . In fact, it probably did him some good."

Mom eyed her patiently. "That's what I mean. Honey, it's obvious you don't care for John and you don't want me spending time with him. But there's really nothing for you to worry about. You certainly don't need to douse him to scare him off."

"Mother!"

"Now, hear me out. Isn't it just possible that you imagined the vampire trying to get in here because, well, because that's kind of how you see John?"

"I don't believe—"

"And maybe that's what made you throw water on him after you saw him."

Becka was speechless. Now her own mother was turning against her! For the millionth time, Becka wished that her father were still alive. Everything was so out of whack, so off balance, with him gone.

She dropped into a chair and crossed her

arms, fixing her mother with a steady gaze. "You're right about one thing. I don't like you being around John."

"You see—"

"I mean, the guy's an obvious sleaze."

"That's exactly what—"

"But I didn't attack him on purpose, Mom. I didn't know it was John when I threw the water. And . . ." She swallowed hard. A lump was rising in her throat, and she wasn't sure why. "I did see something outside that window. You've got to believe me. I really did."

Sensing her emotion, Mom crossed over and put her arm around Becka. "I believe you, sweetheart. I believe you."

Becka nodded. The lump was bigger now. And she could feel her eyes start to burn with moisture. The hug helped a little. But not enough.

∼

If vampires don't exist, who invented them?

Becka sat in front of the computer, waiting for Z's response. If he was so certain vampires didn't exist, then he had better have a pretty good explanation for where the idea first came from.

It was late and she was exhausted. But

she'd gotten Z on-line, and she wasn't about to let him get away.

She waited and watched as his reply came in:

Many believe the legend was invented centuries
ago to enforce proper burial procedures.
The belief was spread that if bodies were buried
in shallow graves they could come back
to life as the "undead."

Becka leaned over and typed:

So people started digging deeper graves?

Z answered:

Precisely. Bram Stoker added to the myth when
he wrote the horror novel *Dracula*, which was
published one hundred years ago.

But why do people still believe in them today?

There are various theories. A very high percentage
of those who believe in vampires are abused
children and teens who identify strongly with
vampire victims. Noted authorities, like J. Gordon
Melton, believe the resurgence of vampire folklore
comes as a result of AIDS and other interests
and concerns related to human blood.

Becka leaned back in the chair and stared at the screen. The history lesson was good, but it didn't solve any problems. Something very frightening was still going on, and she was in the center of it.

Z clearly did not believe in vampires, and he had never been wrong before.

Never.

Then again, he had not seen what she had seen.

She signed off, shut down the computer, then crossed toward her bed. It was doubtful sleep would come, but she had to try. Somehow she figured tomorrow would be an even bigger day. . . .

~

Thanks to John Barberini, stories about the lead actress of a movie being stalked by a vampire had already reached the American press. Gossipy news shows like *Media Tonight* and *Inside Scoop* rushed to send out video crews.

When Becka returned to the set the next morning, everyone seemed a lot more tense. Even the easygoing Tim Paxton seemed on edge. "Hello, Rebecca."

"Hi," she said. She wondered if he'd heard about her own little encounter the night before, but he said nothing. Just as well. The fewer people who thought she was losing her mind, the better.

"Listen," he said, lowering his voice slightly, "I know you're a friend of Jaimie's, so I'd appreciate it if you would try to help keep her calm today."

"What do you mean?"

"Well, she's got a couple of very important interviews to do tonight, and I don't want her to seem . . . well, too off the wall, if you know what I mean."

Becka nodded. "Sure, I'll do what I can. Hey, have you seen Ryan?"

"He was with Jaimie by the prop truck the last time I saw him."

"Tim!" It was Fallon, shouting from the set. "Tim? Anybody seen my producer?!"

Tim finished his coffee with a gulp. "Duty calls." With that he turned and strode toward the director, who was obviously having another one of his hissy fits.

Becka shook her head and watched in amusement. Showbiz. What weird people.

Moments later she meandered through the busy set toward the prop trailer. As she approached, she could hear Jaimie's voice from behind the trailer.

"You don't understand," Jaimie was saying. "At night these wounds in my neck throb and ache, and somehow I know that the only way it'll stop is if I go out . . . and find him."

"I won't let that happen," Ryan replied. "I won't let anything hurt you. I . . . I love you."

Becka stopped in her tracks as if someone had slugged her in the gut. She suddenly felt very weak. She had to lean against the prop trailer for support. So it was true; her worst fears were confirmed.

"But what if I'm turning?" Jaimie's voice continued. "What if I'm becoming one of them?"

"That won't happen," Ryan insisted. "We won't let it happen."

Jaimie's voice trembled now, as if she were holding back her tears. "But what if it already did?"

A long moment of silence passed. Becka felt tears well up in her own eyes.

At last Ryan spoke. "If that happens, I might as well be your first victim . . . because I don't want to go on without you."

That was it. Becka could stand no more. "Nooooo!" she shouted as she raced around the trailer to confront the two.

As soon as she saw them, Becka realized her mistake. Ryan was sitting on the back steps of the trailer with a script in one hand and a Pepsi in the other. Jaimie sat in a lawn chair a few feet away, sipping iced tea.

They had been rehearsing her lines.

Both turned and stared at Becka. Ryan was

the first to speak. "What's the matter, Beck? You OK?"

She felt less than two feet tall. "I . . . I . . . I thought . . . I mean, I thought . . ."

"You thought we were serious?" Jaimie said, already starting to giggle.

"No, of course not," Becka lied. "I-I was just kidding. . . ."

Of course they knew the truth, and Becka wished she could simply disappear.

Fortunately, a voice came over the loudspeaker. "Attention, cast!" It was the assistant director. "We're almost ready on the set, and Dirk would like everyone here."

"Oh, I've got to go," Jaimie said. "Thanks for going over my lines with me, Ryan." She rose from the chair and straightened her costume. "See you guys later. And don't worry, Becka." She tried to hold back her giggle but didn't quite succeed. "I haven't grown any fangs. Yet."

As Jaimie hurried off toward the set, Becka whispered, "That's a matter of opinion."

Ryan turned to her. "What did you say?"

Becka eyed him coolly. "Nothing. I'm going back to the hotel."

Ryan shrugged. "Suit yourself. But you know, I thought we were supposed to make friends with Jaimie. I mean, I thought that was part of why we were here . . . to help her."

"Well, you've certainly been doing *your* part," Becka replied.

"What does that mean?"

"It means you should have been there with me last night."

"Why? Do you think this thing, whatever it is, would be afraid of me? I doubt it."

Becka heard her voice beginning to crack. She was feeling more emotions than she had thought possible. "I needed you. Don't you understand? I . . ."

Hearing her emotion, Ryan rose to his feet. "I do understand, Beck. Believe me. And I would have given anything to have been there to help." Unsure what to do, he started to cross toward her.

But the tears began to come, and Becka had to turn away. "I . . . I'd better go." With that she started off.

"Becka!" Ryan called after her. "Becka, wait. . . ."

But she kept on walking.

~

Ryan sat in one of the cloth chairs near the set. He wasn't sure what to do. It was just after nightfall. The shooting had wrapped, and Becka still hadn't returned to the set. Should he go after her? See how she was doing? But what about his job? Wasn't he being paid to help Jaimie? And what about Z's instructions to look out for her?

Like Becka's, Ryan's own thoughts seemed to be growing more and more muddled.

"Ryan," Jaimie called out as she headed for the costume trailer, "I'm afraid I have to go to wardrobe and be fitted for something we're adding tomorrow. It shouldn't take too long."

Ryan rose to his feet and joined her. "Do you think I have time to run back to the hotel? I want to check . . ."

Jaimie smiled as his voice trailed off. "Check on Becka?" she asked.

He nodded.

"Sure, go ahead. I'm afraid I'll only have ten or fifteen minutes to grab dinner before tonight's interviews anyway. I'll meet you after the television taping. How does ten sound?"

"Ten will be great." Ryan turned and started for the hotel. "I'll see you then."

ᴎ

Jaimie watched Ryan's rapid departure. She sighed, wondering what it would be like to have someone care about you the way he clearly cared about Becka. She recalled the look on the other girl's face when she had come around the trailer earlier and smiled slightly. Obviously, those two needed to talk.

But she didn't have time to worry about their problems. If she didn't get to the wardrobe trailer in a hurry, she'd have no time for dinner at all. Glancing around, she saw that there were still plenty of people milling around the set. With all these people around, she didn't even think twice about cutting across the darkened area between the two production trucks.

The figure in the shadows watched the young girl's advance and grew eager with anticipation. This was exactly what it wanted. What it had been waiting for.

Jaimie had only taken a couple of steps into the darkness before she paused. She glanced around uneasily, looking over her shoulder and from side to side. It was as though she sensed the presence waiting for her.

The form drew back into the shadows.

The girl shook her head, as though chiding herself for her silliness. She glanced back at the people around the set and then toward the wardrobe trailer. The one watching her gauged her thoughts from her expression. The trailer was less than a hundred yards away. . . . She'd just pass through the brief darkness and be there in an instant.

It smiled.

She moved forward again, but her steps grew more cautious by the second. She carefully eyed the darkness around her.

The form waited. The girl continued drawing closer. In just a matter of seconds . . .

Again, Jaimie slowed to a stop. "Hello . . . ," she called. "Who's there?"

The form remained motionless, not even breathing.

The girl was straining to listen, and the cold smile crept over the watcher's lips again. It knew there was nothing to hear. Nothing but the frightened beating of the girl's heart as her growing fear began to pound in her ears.

Ever so slowly the form crouched, preparing to spring.

The girl drew a breath to steady herself. Then, with resolved determination, she moved forward. Quicker this time, anxious to get out of the dark.

A pity that was not going to happen.

The form attacked.

~

Jaimie had no time to scream. She saw only the glint of white fangs and the evil of yellow eyes. And the hands. The deathly white hands wrapped around her throat.

She struggled, trying to breathe, trying to

scream. But the more she struggled, the
tighter the creature's grip grew. She was
growing light-headed. Things were spinning.
Spots danced in her vision. Everything was
turning white.

And, for a brief instant, as she was passing
out, Jaimie wondered if she would feel the
vampire's teeth enter her neck before she
died.

5

Tim Paxton and
Dirk Fallon were arguing again.

"If we reshoot the scene now," Tim was saying, "it's going to cost as much as a full setup. That set's been down for days."

"I realize that," Fallon replied, "but if we don't reshoot it, we're going to have a hole in the middle of the film the size of the

Grand Canyon. I've seen what we shot last week, Tim, and it's horrible. The girl is terrible."

"Have some compassion," Tim argued. "That was the day this vampire business started."

Fallon began pacing back and forth. "I understand that. But it's you who needs to have the compassion. You're the one who has to give me some slack, get some extra money so I can reshoot."

Tim held up his hands. "All right, all right. Let me talk to Jaimie first. I want her to sit with us and watch the scene. If she can't do any better, then—"

"If she can't do any better," the director's voice rose, "then we all might as well pack up and go home."

"But let's wait until after the interviews tonight," Tim suggested.

Fallon shrugged. "That's your call. But the best time to ask your investors for more money would be right after the thing airs in L.A."

"All right," the producer sighed. "Wait here. I'll go get the girl."

Tim hurried off toward wardrobe. Normally, he would have taken the long way around. He wasn't superstitious, nor was he anything close to a coward, but he'd just as soon avoid the shadows in this crazy country. This time, though, he noticed that the television crews from *Media Tonight* were already gathered in front of one of the trucks. They'd made themselves at home, waiting to set up for their interview later that evening, so he decided to cut behind the trucks rather than work his way through the crowd of media vultures.

He crossed through the shadows and was barely halfway when he saw a form lying off to the side.

A body. Jaimie's body.

He raced to her side and quickly scooped her into his arms. "Somebody help!" he shouted. He rose to his feet, lifting the limp form and stumbling out of the shadows into the light. "Somebody get us some help!"

Pandemonium swept through the set. People shouting. Someone screaming. Others asking, "Is she dead? Is she dead?"

Jaimie was motionless as Tim laid her on a nearby bench. A small trickle of blood ran down her neck. Tim reached out to touch her face, and she moaned softly.

"I need a doctor!" Tim yelled furiously. "Where's that doctor?!"

By the time the doctor arrived, Jaimie had come around. "I don't need to go to the hospital," she insisted.

"I'll be the judge of that," the doctor said. But moments later, after he'd bandaged the wound, he finally agreed with her. "It's just a small cut," he said. "Missed the vein in your neck by a fraction of an inch, thank God."

"Will she be able to do the interviews this evening?" Fallon asked.

Tim turned and gave him a hard look, but the director persisted, this time speaking directly to Jaimie. "We need all the publicity we can get, kid. Lots of exposure in L.A. Should be good for all of us, if you think you can pull it off. . . ."

Jaimie took the glass of water the doctor offered to her. After a long drink, she nodded. "Sure, Dirk. You're the director. Anything you say."

∾

When Ryan and Becka arrived later that evening, they saw the television cameras already taping. And there, on the crew monitor, was Jaimie, a bandage on her neck, still wearing her bloodstained dress.

"I can't really tell you much else," she was saying. "After he grabbed my throat, I lost consciousness pretty fast. I just remember his eyes. And those fangs."

"What happened?" Ryan cried, but he was

quickly shushed by a crew member, who indicated that they were still taping.

"Thank you, Jaimie Baylor," the pretty host
of the show said. Then, turning directly to the
camera, the woman began her wrap-up: "And
so, live from the set of *The Vampire Returns*,
Media Tonight is grateful to this courageous
young actress for talking with us so soon after
her harrowing ordeal. We'll be right back
with scenes from tomorrow's show."

"Cut!" the television director shouted.

As the crew began taking down equipment
and wrapping cable, Ryan quickly worked his
way through the commotion to Jaimie. "Are
you all right?" he asked.

Jaimie shrugged. "To tell you the truth, I
don't know."

Becka moved to join them. She knew she
should feel bad for Jaimie, and she wanted
to be concerned about the poor girl . . . but
as she watched Ryan fawn over her, she
couldn't help feeling resentment.

"You sure you don't need anything?" she
could hear Ryan asking Jaimie. "I could run
over and get you a glass of water."

"I have a glass of water," Jaimie replied.

"I meant a fresh one, a colder glass of
water."

Jaimie smiled. "Ryan, I'm all right. Just stay
here with me for a while."

Watching them together made Becka's stomach tighten.

"All right," Ryan answered. "I'll stay right here by your side all night if you need me to."

Ryan's last remark turned the tightness in Becka's stomach into full-blown nausea. And to make matters worse, she felt terrible for feeling the way she did. Hadn't Z said—no, hadn't the *Bible* said, "Love your enemies"?

Jaimie wasn't even her enemy . . . or was she? Becka watched the girl lean toward Ryan. The nausea continued to grow, until Becka knew she had to get away. Without a word, she turned and headed off in the opposite direction, feeling both angry and guilty.

As she crossed by the catering truck she spotted Maureen, the wardrobe lady, talking with Tim. She slowed to a stop. She didn't mean to eavesdrop. It just turned out that way.

"They should be interviewing *you* over there, Tim," Maureen was saying. "You saved her life. You're a hero."

"I don't know what I did," Tim replied. "I just saw Jaimie and ran to her."

"Well, you scared him off, then."

"Maybe. It happened so fast. I don't even know if I saw him for sure. It was something. Kind of looked like a man . . . but kind of like a . . ."

Maureen was all ears. "A what? What'd it look like?"

Tim shrugged. "I don't know. I told you—it happened so fast. But I caught a glimpse of something. . . . It almost looked like . . . a bat."

"Oh, my. Did you tell the TV people?"

Tim shook his head. "No, I did not. And I don't want you babbling anything like that, either. It sounds crazy enough. Besides, as any producer will tell you, if you want your movie to be a hit, let the actress be the one who gets her face on TV, not some ugly mug like me."

Maureen laughed. Tim noticed Becka then. He excused himself and walked over to her. "Hello, Becka."

She swallowed. "Hi. Listen, I didn't mean to eavesdrop, but—"

"That's OK. Did you hear what I was saying?" Becka nodded.

"Then do me a favor, will you?"

"What's that?"

"Don't say anything to Jaimie about that bat business. She's got enough on her mind already."

Becka looked at him and slowly nodded.

∿

"A bat!" Ryan's face was incredulous. "He said it turned into a bat?"

"That's what he said," Becka insisted. They tried to relax in the living room of her hotel suite later that night. "Of course, Tim said he wasn't sure," she continued. "It happened so fast, but . . ."

Ryan paced around the small room.

She could tell he was concerned and tried her best to be sincere. "How was Jaimie?"

Ryan sighed. "OK, I guess. Tim and two of the stunt guys are camping out in her suite."

"Listen," Becka said, "I'm sorry I walked off the set earlier today. I sort of lost it, and I . . . well, I just felt foolish, that's all."

"No problem," Ryan replied, "but I . . ." His voice trailed off.

"What?"

Ryan shook his head. "Nothing."

"Tell me," she said.

"All right. It's just that . . . I got worried about you and . . . I left Jaimie to check on you . . . and that's when she was attacked."

"Too bad." Becka couldn't keep the sarcasm out of her voice.

"I don't mean anything by it," Ryan tried to explain. "I just feel kind of bad, that's all."

Becka heard her voice becoming icy. "That's nice. It's just too bad I wasn't the one attacked instead."

"That's not what I meant!" Ryan protested.

An awkward silence passed between them.

Becka couldn't help noticing that there had been a lot of those lately.

Finally, Ryan spoke. "I heard half the crew was out looking to buy more crucifixes."

Becka nodded. "I heard worse. Some of them are planning on wearing garlic because it's supposed to ward off vampires."

"This is crazy," Ryan said. He resumed his pacing. "If someone had told me what was happening here, I wouldn't have believed it."

"I know what you mean."

"And talk about crucifixes," Ryan continued. "You should see what Tim and those stunt guys have up in Jaimie's suite. It looks like they bought out the store."

"What are we going to do?" Becka said. "I mean, no one is doing anything that really makes sense. It's like they're just sitting around waiting for the vampire to attack again."

Ryan nodded. "We're always on the defensive. Maybe it's time to start playing offense."

"What do you mean?"

"I'm not sure. Maybe set a trap . . . try to catch the vampire."

Becka was intrigued. "How?"

"Well, I was thinking—" Ryan grew more excited as he spoke—"if we could lure him into a dead-end alley or someplace like that, then we could jump out with a bunch of holy water and crucifixes and—"

"And do what?" Becka asked sarcastically. "Drive a stake through his heart?"

"I don't know," Ryan said, completely missing her humor. "I doubt I'm up to that. But at least we could get a better idea of what we're fighting."

Becka let out a long sigh of frustration. She knew Ryan was a fairly new Christian, but it was like he'd forgotten everything they'd learned about spiritual warfare. If this thing was real, and she was growing more and more certain it was, then the way to fight it was the same way they had fought other attacks of the enemy: through prayer and the Word of God.

"Listen," she said sincerely, "I'm not crazy about using crucifixes, holy water, and all that folktale stuff to fight this thing."

He paused. "I know."

"Ryan, if we do anything, it should be to pray. If there really is some sort of demonic force involved, then we should be fighting it with prayer."

Ryan nodded slowly. "OK, I'll blast him with holy water while you pray."

Becka protested, "Ryan . . ."

"Listen," he explained. "The thing about folktales is that there's usually some truth to them."

"I know, but—"

"I just want to *do* something," he continued. "I mean, we can pray if you want, but I really don't think this other stuff will hurt, do you?"

Becka shrugged. Maybe he had a point. "OK," she agreed reluctantly. "If that's what you want. But if we're going to pray, we'd better do it now, 'cause things aren't getting any better."

Ryan agreed and moved to sit beside her. Together the two bowed their heads and began to pray.

Becka loved these times. As a new Christian, Ryan always prayed with freshness and excitement. And he was honest. Very, very honest. Despite his weaknesses and his total cluelessness about Jaimie, his honesty always tugged at and captured Becka's heart.

Together they prayed for several minutes, asking God for wisdom about what to do, confessing their doubts and weaknesses, and asking for God's protection over Jaimie and themselves, regardless of what they were dealing with. But there was one thing Becka would not, *could not,* do. She did not ask for God's help to love Jaimie.

They'd barely finished when Mom opened the door to the suite.

"Becka, sweetheart," she said as she entered the room, "John told me what happened to Jaimie. I came back as quickly as I could. Is she all right?"

"I think so," Becka said.

"How are you?"

Becka stared at her for a moment before answering. How was she? Between her frustration over Jaimie's vampire, her anger over a beautiful Hollywood actress practically throwing herself at Ryan, and her mother hanging around with an obvious creep, Becka definitely felt the stress.

"I'm just fine," she said, doing her best to hide the tension in her voice. But even she could hear how harsh and sarcastic the words sounded.

"Would you like to talk about it?" her mother asked quietly.

"No, Mom. It's OK. Really." She sighed again. "I think I'm just tired." Tired of Jaimie. Tired of Ryan paying more attention to a girl he'd just met than to the one who was supposed to be his closest friend. Tired of feeling angry and jealous and guilty.

"Well," Ryan said after an uneasy silence filled the room, "it's getting late. Let's get together first thing tomorrow and start working out a plan."

Becka nodded and walked him to the door. But even then a thought came to her

mind. "We've still got one major problem
with any plan we use to trap the vampire."

Ryan paused at the door. "What's that?"

"We may have everything we need to try to
trap the thing, but . . ."

"But what?"

Becka took a deep breath and slowly let it
out. "Every trap needs bait."

~

The next day even Dirk Fallon acknowledged
that filming another vampire attack on
Jaimie might not be a wise idea. Not after all
she had been through the night before. So
instead they chose to film the scene in the
movie where Van Helsing reveals who the
vampire really is.

They were filming in an old mansion not
far from the hotel when Rebecca and Ryan
arrived. They'd spent several hours that
morning carefully hatching a plan and
visiting the location where they hoped the
capture would take place. They would
explain it all to Jaimie when she was done
with the scene, but for now, they watched
silently as Steve Delton prepared to confront the actor playing the movie's vampire.

"So, gentlemen," Van Helsing said, "I ask
you to consider who among this esteemed

group of lords and ladies could possibly be such an abomination."

The other three men shrugged their shoulders, clearly at a loss. Jaimie sat in the far corner of the room, listening intently.

Van Helsing was obviously enjoying his moment in the spotlight. "No opinions among such learned men as yourselves? I'm surprised. All right, then. But first, I ask, are you aware of the three tests of being a vampire?"

It was about then that Becka felt as if someone was staring at her. She turned and was surprised to see Dirk Fallon, the director, looking in her direction.

What's he doing watching me instead of the scene? she thought. *Does he know what Ryan and I are up to?*

She figured it was unlikely, but she also knew he made her very nervous, staring like that. In fact, she felt so uncomfortable that if Van Helsing had asked her who the vampire was, she probably would have pointed at the film's director.

She looked back to the scene as Van Helsing explained his three tests. First, the vampire could not endure sunlight. Second, he would feel physical pain if he came in contact with a crucifix or other holy object. And finally, vampires cast no reflections.

Becka turned back toward Fallon.

He kept watching her.

She tried to force a smile and nodded. But as soon as she did, he turned away as if he hadn't been looking.

What was he thinking? What did he know?

"So," Van Helsing was saying, "test one requires the sunlight. It is now night. And since I cannot go among the guests here and spray holy water or touch them with crucifixes, I have done the next best thing. If you will look to your left you will see that I had the large mirror over the mantel rehung this afternoon. It now reflects anyone entering this room from the parlor."

The other characters in the scene mumbled their acknowledgment, and Van Helsing nodded to someone near the door. "I have asked Mr. Scott to call all of the guests into this room to hear an announcement. Watch the mirror carefully, gentlemen."

Why can't it be this easy in real life? Becka thought. *Too bad we couldn't just carry a mirror around until we found who the vampire was.* Obviously it couldn't be anyone in the cast or crew, since they were all out in the daylight. But then, who knew if vampires' fear of daylight was myth or reality? Maybe it was the same about casting reflections. Maybe none of what anyone thought was true. Maybe it was all folklore.

She threw a glance back over to the director. He was now watching the scene. Good.

Steve Delton, the actor playing Van Helsing, continued.

"But one more thing, gentlemen—remember that the vampire is a creature of the night and draws his strength from the dark realm. The only sure way to protect yourself is to stay in the light. Unfortunately—and this is what makes our situation so intriguing—you will never catch him unless you venture into the dark."

All was quiet for a second, and then Fallon yelled, "Cut! Print that one."

The assistant director shouted, "Half hour cast break. Crew, set up Scene 72 in the parlor."

Becka and Ryan exchanged nods. It was time to tell Jaimie their plan. They turned and walked toward her. Up close, the girl looked drawn and pale. In fact, she looked so bad that for a moment Becka had second thoughts about even telling her what they had in mind.

But they had to do something. If the vampire—or whatever it was—was to be stopped, this was the time to stop it.

"Hey, guys," Jaimie called out when she saw them.

"How are you feeling?" Becka asked.

Jaimie smiled. "Worse than I look, if you can believe that."

"You look great," Ryan lied.

"Thank you." Jaimie almost laughed. "I'm grateful for the compliment, even if I don't believe it."

Ryan smiled, obviously caught. "Listen . . . Becka and I were talking last night, and it seems like it's time to change our tactics on this vampire thing."

"What do you mean?"

"Well, up to now, none of us wanted to believe it was real, so we just kept sitting around, waiting for it to attack. Now . . . well, maybe it's time we start fighting back."

Jaimie's eyes widened. "How?"

"By trapping him," Ryan explained. "We could set up some place, like in a dead end, and get all our antivampire stuff together there. Then we could lure it in there and spring the trap."

Jaimie looked puzzled. "But how do we get him to go into the alley?"

Becka and Ryan exchanged looks. Ryan cleared his throat. "Well, uh, we have to make him think that something he wants is, well, that it's there. Then when he—"

Jaimie still looked confused. "Something he wants. What does he want?"

After a long pause Ryan finally answered. "You, Jaimie. He wants you."

If Jaimie had been pale before, she was downright white now.

"You wouldn't actually have to stay there," Ryan explained. "We'd set it up so you could get out while he stayed trapped."

"There's a dead-end alley a few blocks from here," Becka added. "If we get him inside the alley and block off the front, the only way out is at the end of the alley through a steel door that leads to a warehouse."

"So," Ryan's voice grew more excited, "the plan is for you to go down the alley. And when the vampire comes, one of us will block the entrance to the alley while the other one opens the door to the warehouse to let you escape. Then we quickly close the door before he can follow, and he's trapped in the alley."

Jaimie looked doubtful. "He'll break through the door."

Becka shook her head. "He can't. It's solid steel with two locks and a crossbar."

"You've checked this out already?" Jaimie asked.

Becka nodded. "It's called Dominski Containers, or something like that."

"It has a steel fire door," Ryan said. "I'm sure the manager will let us use it if Tim or someone from the film company asks."

Jaimie listened as Ryan outlined the rest of the plan. "After the vampire enters the alley, we'll block the entrance with crosses and water—

"I thought you said Becka didn't believe in that stuff," Jaimie interrupted.

"I don't," Becka said. "That's why we're also throwing in a big production truck to block the alley for good measure."

Jaimie still wasn't convinced. "Where will you get the truck?"

"Tim," Ryan answered. "There's no way we can pull this off without his help."

"I see," Jaimie said. "OK, but no one except Tim should know about this."

Ryan and Becka agreed.

Slowly, a smile came over Jaimie's face. "I guess it's a pretty foolproof plan, huh?"

Becka nodded. "As far as we can tell."

"That's good, Becka," Jaimie said, looking her straight in the eyes. "Because if it doesn't work, *I'm* the one who will be at a dead end."

6

At first Tim stared at Becka and Ryan like they'd lost their minds when they approached him about using the warehouse entrance and the production truck.

"You're kidding," he said. "A couple of teenage kids want to trap a vampire?"

"We're doing it for Jaimie," Ryan replied.

"It's only a matter of time before he gets to her again."

Tim shook his head. "I've got people with Jaimie around the clock. And they're armed with every bit of vampire defense we can find."

"Yes, but those are all defensive measures," Becka said.

"That's right," Ryan said. "We can't just wait. We have to go on the offense."

Tim looked at them a moment, then nodded slowly. "All right, what have we got to lose? Except my leading actress, of course. But listen, I want you kids to keep this quiet. Half of Hollywood thinks I'm nuts already. I'll help you, I'll even drive the truck, but until we catch this thing, let's keep it between us and Jaimie."

"Agreed," Becka said.

"OK," Ryan added, "but somehow we have to put the word out that Jaimie will be there."

"We've still got another alley scene to shoot. She can be rehearsing for it there. No one will question that. But someone will have to go over the lines with her to make it look good."

"That's perfect," Ryan exclaimed. "Jaimie and I will be rehearsing alone in the alley. Then, when we think the time is right, I'll leave as if I'm going to get us a can of pop or something, and Jaimie will wait there alone."

"I could be standing just inside the warehouse door," Becka said.

"And I'll head down the block like I'm leaving," Ryan continued. "But then I'll double back, and when the vampire goes into the alley, we spring the trap."

Becka nodded. "As soon as the vampire starts toward Jaimie, I'll throw open the door and pull Jaimie inside, where it's safe."

"Meanwhile," Tim said, "I'll be waiting in the truck. And when he goes into the alley, I'll quickly back up and block the entrance."

"Right," Ryan agreed. "As soon as I pour the water, you start the truck. And when I get the crucifixes all laid down, you back it up."

The thought of using superstitious solutions still made Becka uneasy, but Ryan seemed so set on them. . . .

"I'll put the word out as soon as we fill Jaimie in on the plan," Tim said. "It sounds pretty foolproof. Simple and straightforward."

But even as he finished the sentence, a worried silence settled over the group. What would happen to Jaimie if they failed?

"It's not a bad plan," Ryan offered.

It was Becka who said what they were all feeling: "For Jaimie's sake, it had better be a great one."

"This place gives me the creeps," Rebecca said as the front door to the warehouse creaked open. "I'm glad you're here with me."

"It's not so bad," Tim said, shining his flashlight around the room. "It's just old."

It was a little after seven o'clock, and most of the cast and crew were at dinner. Word had spread that rehearsals for the upcoming alley scene would take place in the alley next to the Dominski warehouse. Tim had worked out an arrangement with the manager and had even sent a couple of electricians over to the alley to rig up some rehearsal lights. Then, while everyone else was eating dinner, he drove one of the production trucks over to the front of the alley. Once it was in position, he and Becka entered the warehouse.

After fumbling for the light switch, Tim finally turned it on. "There. Not so bad, huh?"

Shiny metal rectangles hanging from large wooden pegs on the wall filled the front part of the musty old shop. Some of the rectangles were copper, some were bronze, some polished chrome, but all were about the same size. "Wonder what these are for," Becka said as they walked by.

"They look like handles to me," Tim said.

"Yeah, that's what they are. See, this piece here fits over the rectangle, and the other end attaches to the box."

"What box?" Becka asked as they rounded the corner toward the part of the shop that faced the alley. She hesitated a moment. It was dark in there, and she wasn't about to go in first.

"Don't you know?" Tim said as he turned the corner, shining his flashlight. Becka waited as he took a couple more steps into the room. "Didn't you see this place before?"

"Not really," Becka said. "I just talked to the manager about it. When he showed me the door, we were outside in the alley."

"So you don't know what they make here?" Tim said as he reached the wall, searching for the light switch. As he did, his flashlight exposed glimpses of metal boxes stacked about the room.

"I tried to look up the word that comes after Dominski on the sign out front in the hotel bookstore, but the closest I got was some kind of container. I figured it's the Dominski Container Company or something like that."

"Close," Tim said as he found the light switch and turned it on. "It's the Dominski Casket Company."

Becka's mouth dropped open. All around

her were stacks and stacks of metal caskets. All sizes and types, waiting to be shipped out.

"Listen," Tim said, "I'd better be going."

"What?" Becka croaked. "Can't you stay, you know . . . a little longer?"

There was no missing the amusement in Tim's voice. "You'll be OK, kid. Ryan and Jaimie will be heading into the alley any second. I've got to take my post inside the truck before someone sees me."

Becka forced herself to swallow and tried to nod. As long as the light was on, she didn't feel too bad. Still, she found herself whispering a quiet prayer that the caskets with their long lids wouldn't suddenly start popping open.

"OK, then." Tim turned and started for the door. "I'll be shutting these lights off now and—"

"Shutting the lights off?" Becka interrupted, her voice cracking even more.

"I have to. You can see the light under the door from the alley. It could scare him off before we even spring the trap."

"I'm not too worried about scaring *him* off," Becka said. "He doesn't seem like he'd be that easily scared."

"True," Tim said. "But a vampire's senses are supposed to be highly attuned, so we'd better be extra careful."

Becka wanted to say something, but at the moment she didn't much trust her voice.

Seeing the expression on her face, Tim reached into his satchel. "Don't worry," he said, "I brought an extra flashlight."

Becka gratefully accepted it, but as Tim turned off the lights and left, she began to shiver. She tried to tell herself it was just the cold, but of course she knew better.

The front door closed with a dull thud. The sound echoed about the caskets.

She was all alone. Everything was silent.

For a moment she thought she heard something. A quiet rustling over in the far corner.

Probably just a rat, she thought. But for some reason, the idea gave her little comfort.

Then there were the coffin lids. What would happen if one or two or a dozen started opening?

Maybe it was her overactive imagination, or maybe it was the rodents she heard scampering around the coffins, but more than once she thought she saw moving shadows.

Of course, when she shined her light in that direction, she saw nothing.

She just hoped it would stay that way.

Carefully, she approached the inside of the alley door, shining her light over every square inch of floor in front of her.

She could see a small slot between the bars on the door and pressed her face against it to peer through and view a small portion of the alley. The lights the crew had rigged up cast a dim glow outside, but the shadows over-powered the light.

Becka took a breath to steady herself and wondered when Ryan and Jaimie would show. Her heart pounded already, and they'd barely begun. She wanted this whole thing to be over as quickly as possible. In fact, she wished she had never even given in to the plan.

There was another noise behind her. Faint scampering.

She spun the flashlight around, but nothing was there. The strange noises worried her the most. And, of course, the caskets. And, of course, the shadows she kept thinking she saw move atop them.

Then she heard scraping gravel. And voices.

Becka eased closer to the door. Through the slot, she could see Ryan and Jaimie approaching.

Finally.

As they approached, Jaimie rehearsed her lines. Pretending to be the character in the film, she walked through the alley with a slight swirl and sashay. It was easy to imagine her in the long and flowing dress she would wear in the actual filming.

"Why are you so shy, David?" she said, hardly glancing at the script. "Do you no longer desire me because of my wounds?"

For a moment there was silence as Ryan fumbled for his place in the script. "Of course I do," he finally said, slightly overacting his part. "It's just that I . . . I don't want to . . ."

"Well, come closer, then," Jaimie cooed.

Becka felt herself bristle at the sound of Jaimie's voice. Even now, as they waited for the vampire, it was obvious that the girl was coming on to Ryan.

And she *knew* Becka was watching.

Becka could see Ryan moving next to Jaimie. His voice caught as he spoke. "My feelings haven't changed, but I don't want to take advantage of you. I don't want—"

"You're not taking advantage of me," Jaimie said. And with that she reached up and caressed Ryan's cheek.

As Becka watched the scene, her anger grew. Did Jaimie really have to pick this scene to rehearse? And did she really have to touch Ryan like that?

As if reading her thoughts, Ryan cast a glance toward the door. "I . . . uh, I only hope that we can resume our romance the way it was before that terrible attack on you."

Jaimie took a step toward him and reached up to slide her arm around his neck.

Becka couldn't believe her eyes. The girl was about to kiss him!

But at the last second Ryan backed off.

"What are you doing?" Jaimie asked.

Ryan fumbled through his script, looking for the line.

Jaimie shook her head. "Ryan, what are you doing? You're not supposed to pull away. This is where I bite your neck."

"It is?" Ryan looked confused.

"Yes, this is where I start to cross over and become a vampire. You don't pull away until you feel my lips on your neck. . . . *Then* you pull back."

"Oh yeah, uh, OK." Ryan nodded.

For a brief moment Becka thought about throwing open the alley door, grabbing Ryan, and letting the real vampire attack Jaimie. Her self-control got the better of her, but barely.

"You know what?" Ryan spoke just a little too loudly, as if he wanted to be overheard. "I'm pretty thirsty. Do you mind if I get something to drink?"

He was moving to the next step of the plan. Becka glanced at her watch. It was a few minutes earlier than they had scheduled, but for obvious reasons she was grateful he had decided to move things up.

Jaimie said what she was supposed to say, "All right . . . but would you be a dear and bring something back for me? I want to block out the scene a bit on my own. You know, walk it through and decide where I'm going to say what."

"Sure," Ryan said, once again just a little too loudly. "I'll run down to that store in the next block and be right back. You'll be OK . . . all alone . . . the only one here in the alley."

Becka almost smiled. Ryan was doing his best, but Tom Cruise he wasn't.

"I'll be fine," Jaimie said.

"OK," Ryan said. "I am leaving now. Don't worry; you will be all right." With that he turned and headed down the alley.

It was time for Becka to make her move. Carefully, and ever so quietly, she unbolted the alley door so she could fling it open and yank Jaimie in when the vampire attacked.

She glanced down at her fingers and noticed they were already trembling.

Outside in the alley, Jaimie pretended to rehearse her lines as she walked and paced out the scene.

Other than her soft tones and the slightest

scuff of her shoes in the alley, everything was very quiet.

The trap was set and waiting.

Then Becka heard it. A dragging, shuffling kind of sound. Something moved down the alley in their direction.

She grabbed the door handle and held her breath.

Through the crack, she could see Jaimie's body tense. She'd heard the sound, too.

The noise stopped.

Jaimie lowered her voice to a mere whisper as she recited her lines, pretending she hadn't heard.

A full minute passed, and everything remained silent.

Maybe he'd moved on. Maybe he'd sensed it was a trap.

Jaimie turned and stole a look up the alley. Becka heard her gasp, then saw her draw her hand up to her mouth.

He was there!

Jaimie, who was several yards from the warehouse door, began backing up.

"Who are you?" she called out. "What do you want from me?"

Becka could hear nothing in reply. The vampire did not respond. Instead, the scraping of gravel resumed.

It was approaching.

Becka scrunched to the side for a better look but could see nothing.

More scuffing sounded as Jaimie continued backing up toward the warehouse door.

It was obvious the vampire was moving in.

Then through the crack, in the shadowy light, Becka saw him! The same creature she had seen attack Jaimie in the alley their first night in Transylvania. The same creature she had seen suspended in midair outside her hotel window.

Jaimie continued backing toward the door, only eight feet away now.

The vampire appeared to be in no hurry. In fact, he matched her step for step. Every time she took a step backward, he took a step forward.

Jaimie glanced toward the door. It was obvious she was thinking of making a run for it. It was also obvious that at this distance the vampire could overtake her before she made it.

In the dim shadows, Becka could see Jaimie starting to tremble. She wondered if the girl would even have the strength to take the last remaining steps.

"W-why . . . ," Jaimie stuttered. "Why are you doing this? Why me?" Her voice cracked with each syllable.

But the vampire did not answer. He did not even blink his fierce yellow eyes.

He just kept approaching.

She was five steps away now.

Becka's grip tightened on the door. Any second now.

There! There it was. The sound of a truck starting up!

The vampire spun around.

Becka pressed against the door for a better look. In the distance she could see Ryan's form spring into view. He dumped the large pitcher of water across the alley entrance.

The vampire growled, distracted.

This was the moment. Now Jaimie was to break for the door. But she appeared paralyzed, unable to move.

"Come on, Jaimie," Becka whispered. "Move! Get closer. Get closer."

Jaimie stumbled backward another step. Then another.

Good. She was within reaching distance.

It was now or never. Becka slammed against the door to throw it open.

But it was stuck!

She threw her shoulder into it again.

It wouldn't budge.

She pushed harder, banging against it with all of her might.

It didn't move.

"Rebecca!" It was Jaimie. Crying for help. She had arrived at the door and was banging on it. "Let me in!"

Becka panicked. Through the slot she saw the vampire make his move. His cape billowing out behind him like giant wings, he started toward the girl.

"Becka!"

Becka slammed against the door again.

Jaimie continued banging. *"Help me!"*

Then Becka saw it. One of the bolts was still locked in place. With trembling hands she clumsily pushed it aside and threw open the door.

The vampire was nearly there.

Jaimie screamed as Becka grabbed her and yanked her inside.

She reached for the door to pull it shut, and for a brief second, she stood face-to-face with the vampire. He was three feet away, reaching for her. His eyes glowed with hate. She pulled the door with all of her might.

It slammed shut with a loud thud . . . which was immediately followed by another thud as the vampire slammed into the door.

Becka fumbled with the bolts, sliding them into place.

"There!" she cried.

SLAM!

The vampire hit the door again with such

force that she thought she saw the steel actually give a little.

Both girls turned and raced toward the front of the warehouse. They flew down the hall, running for their lives as the vampire slammed into the door a third time.

Within seconds, they made it to the other side of the shop and out the front entrance to the street.

Immediately Becka spotted Ryan laying down the last of the dozen crosses. He jumped out of the way just as Tim finished parking the truck, sealing off the alley. Tim climbed out of the truck and yelled, "You girls OK?"

Becka nodded and shouted, "Have you got him?"

"We've got him," Tim shouted as he headed around the front of the truck. "He can't get out."

"Let's take a look," Ryan said.

The alley was completely blocked by the long truck, so they had to crawl over the front bumper to squeeze inside.

"Where is he?" Becka asked. She was more than a little nervous as she arrived at Ryan's side.

Their eyes scanned the dim alley. There was no sign of the vampire. Anywhere.

"Look at that door," Ryan said, motioning

down the alley to the steel door. "It's really bent up."

"Shine your lights in all the dark areas," Tim ordered. "Make sure he's not hiding."

Both Becka and Ryan pointed their flashlights into all the shadows.

Nothing.

"Wait!" Ryan yelled. "Over to the left. Something's moving!"

Becka moved her beam to join his. He was right. Something was moving in the shadows.

Suddenly their beams caught it in the light.

"It's a bat!" Tim cried.

And it was. Exposed now and in the light. The creature's wingspan was nearly a yard wide, and the thing flew straight at them.

"Duck!" Becka shouted.

Jaimie screamed as they all hit the pavement.

But the giant bat rose and headed over the truck. They spun around and watched it fly high over their heads and deep into the night.

Everyone was breathing hard, but it was Ryan who finally spoke. "We lost him."

"And he was real," Becka said, shaking her head in amazement. "There's no question about it now. He's a real vampire."

7

The words hung on the screen for what seemed like an endless length of time.

Vampires do not exist.

Rebecca simply stared at them. She couldn't believe Z was so stubborn. It reminded her of

the arguments she used to have with her dad.
Back when he was alive. Back when he knew
he was right and stuck to his guns regardless
of what she said.

She had just finished telling Z about their
failure at trapping the vampire and how the
monster had turned into a bat. Still, despite
all of this evidence, Z insisted there were no
such things as vampires.

She was more than a little frustrated and
wasn't sure what to type next.

Z saved her the trouble.

Did you see him turn into a bat?

I told you he disappeared.

Z remained unimpressed.

Disappeared where?

Becka could feel her ears growing hot
with anger. Why was he giving her the third
degree? Couldn't he just accept that he was
wrong? Furiously, she typed back:

*He either disappeared into thin air . . .
or else he turned into a bat!*

There was a long pause. Becka drummed
her fingers on the desk, waiting impatiently
for Z's response.

Finally, it came:

Look for another explanation.

Becka's fingers flew over the keyboard:

I GAVE you the only explanation!

The reply slowly formed on the screen:

Don't you find it strange that no one has been
seriously injured? Vampires are supposed to be
violent, vicious creatures. Their lust for blood is
unparalleled. As is their strength. Would not a
real vampire have killed someone by now?

What's that supposed to mean?

The only true power this enemy has is the power
of fear. Doesn't the pattern seem familiar?

Becka stared at the screen, trying to understand. Z went on:

Occult activity—whether real, imagined,
or counterfeit—is always based on fear.
In every case, it becomes a matter of choice
to either trust in God's power and experience
his love or to believe in the enemy's
power and live in his fear.

Becka read carefully, beginning to understand. Suddenly, Z changed the subject:

> How are Jaimie and Ryan doing?

Becka felt anger surge through her. Talk about having your buttons pushed! Almost before she could stop herself she punched back:

> *We're talking about vampires,*
> *not Jaimie and Ryan.*

Z's answer returned:

> It's the same enemy.

Becka caught her breath. Z *did* know something. But what was he talking about? What did he mean, "It's the same enemy"? Quickly she typed:

> *Explain.*

> Your fear is leading you to make wrong
> conclusions about the "vampire." Your
> fear of losing Ryan is making you jealous
> and unable to love Jaimie.

Becka's mouth hung open as she reread the words. But Z wasn't finished:

Remember, "God has not given us a spirit of fear."
As you love and trust God, your fear will vanish,
allowing you to think more clearly about this so-
called vampire. As you ask God to help you love
Jaimie, your jealousy over her will also disappear.

Becka continued to stare, barely breathing.
He had done it again. Almost effortlessly, he
had cut past all the surface issues and gone
straight to the heart of the matter.

More words appeared:

> Please check in with me once a day
> so I won't worry.

Becka frowned. If Z was so sure there was
no vampire, then what was he worried about?
As if he were reading her mind, the answer
appeared on the screen:

> Danger comes in many forms. Remember
> Christ's words, "I am with you always."
> This you can believe. Z

Rebecca disconnected and shut down the
computer, her mind spinning.

~

Media people swarmed the set at nightfall
when Becka finally stopped by. By now the

major TV stations had caught the buzz and had sent crews to Transylvania. Everywhere Becka looked, she saw a camera or a microphone.

"Excuse me?"

Becka turned. A handsome man in his early thirties approached. "Are you connected with the film?" he asked.

Before she could answer, he continued. "I was hoping I could get a few comments for American television about this vampire business."

Becka shook her head. The last thing in the world she wanted was to be seen by a zillion people. After all, she was Becka Williams, the girl who did her best to blend into the wallpaper whenever she was in a crowd.

When she didn't respond, the reporter moved on without so much as a nod. Clearly Becka was of no use to him, so he acted as if she didn't exist.

Becka only shook her head, marveling at the rudeness.

The crowd was largest near the food wagon, and as Becka made her way to the counter, she discovered why. There, in the center of about twenty reporters, sat Jaimie. Ryan stood right next to her, trying to act as if he really belonged.

Becka bit her lip and closed her eyes. How could she fight off her jealousy when every time she turned around something like this happened?

Finally, she turned to the man behind the counter. "Mike," she asked, "can I have a cheeseburger?"

He shook his head. "Sorry, got nothing left. Media people cleaned me out. It was even worse at lunch. Unless you want a microwaved burrito or a pepperoni stick."

Becka rolled her eyes. "Thanks, but no thanks."

He nodded and chuckled. "I know what you mean."

She threw another look to Ryan, hoping to get his attention, but he was too busy playing Mr. Hollywood to see her—or, as far as she could tell, to even care that she existed anymore.

Trying not to feel sorry for herself but failing miserably, Becka headed over to the set of the old mansion where they were finishing up the scene she'd watched yesterday.

When she arrived, Van Helsing was about to confront the vampire.

"Excuse me, sir," Van Helsing said to the vampire, "but I noticed you made a rather quick exit from the drawing room. Is there something wrong?"

"No, Dr. Van Helsing," the vampire replied. "Everything is fine."

"I am at a disadvantage," Van Helsing countered. "You seem to know my name, but I do not know yours."

"Everyone knows of the great Dr. Van Helsing," the vampire retorted. "Your reputation is well known here in Transylvania. And as for being at a disadvantage, sir, you are more right than you could ever imagine."

With that, the vampire turned and raced for the door.

"After him!" Van Helsing shouted. "He's the one!"

The men bolted after the vampire, and Dirk Fallon yelled, "Cut!"

Everyone relaxed, and the director shouted, "OK, once again. Places everyone. That was just a little stiff."

"I thought you *wanted* stiff," Steve Delton said.

"I want stiff, Steve," the director called, "but not dead, all right?"

As the actors took their positions, Becka caught a glimpse of Ryan and Jaimie arriving. Apparently they had just finished the interview. Reluctantly, she raised her hand to get their attention. "Ryan, Jaimie . . ."

"Quiet on the set!" Fallon shouted, and Becka wondered if he meant it especially for her. Feeling a little embarrassed, she moved around the outside of the group until she met up with Ryan and Jaimie. They stood next to one of the soundmen, who was wearing headphones and watching the meters on a tape recorder.

"Hey, Becka," Ryan whispered. "Where have you been?" He was his usual good-natured self, as if nothing had happened.

"I . . . I talked to Z," Becka said, although she didn't really want to discuss it in front of Jaimie.

"What'd he say we should do?" Ryan asked in excitement.

Becka shook her head. "That's just it. . . . He says there's no such thing as a vampire."

"What?" Ryan seemed surprised. "Didn't you tell him about the bat?"

"I told him about everything," Becka said sharply. "But he said that no one has been seriously hurt, so—"

"What about the attack on Jaimie?" Ryan interrupted. It was obvious that he was upset. "If Tim hadn't come by then, she'd have been a goner."

"I know, I know," Becka said. "You don't have to convince me."

Ryan set his jaw and scowled. "Well . . . then we'll have to figure out how to beat this thing without Z's help."

"Quiet, please," the soundman said, motioning to the scene that was about to begin.

As before, Van Helsing confronted the vampire, but this time Dirk Fallon yelled "Cut!" before they even finished the scene.

"I'm not buying the vampire running away like that," Fallon said. "I want him to turn slowly and walk toward the door. Then let's have one of the men, the guy in the blue waistcoat, grab on to the vampire's cape. I want the vampire to swat him away, like you'd swat a bug, and then just walk out into the night."

"Do I still shout out that 'After him!' line?" Steve Delton asked.

Fallon shook his head. "No, tend to your friend instead. After the vampire smacks him, he falls into that big wooden cabinet and onto the floor. Can you do that, Blue Waistcoat?" he asked. "Bang into the cabinet and fall to the floor?"

The extra in the blue waistcoat nodded.

"OK, then," Fallon said. "When he falls to the ground, everybody crowd around while Van Helsing attends to him. Clear?"

Everyone nodded.

"All right, then, let's go."

"Quiet on the set," the assistant director yelled. "Have we got tape?"

"We've got tape," the soundman replied.

"OK, roll it!" he shouted to the cameraman.

"Rolling."

The clapboard indicated the scene, and Fallon yelled, "Action!"

As requested, the extra in the blue waistcoat leaped ahead and grabbed the vampire's cape. The vampire turned and grabbed the man's hand. Then, with one great toss, he flung the man backward into the cabinet. Only, instead of slamming against the cabinet and falling to the floor, the extra hit the cabinet too hard, causing it to rock backward. As it did so, one of the doors flew open.

And out toppled a dead man.

Two large bite marks showed on his throat, and he appeared to be totally drained of blood.

8

The crew gasped, and Jaimie screamed as the dead man tumbled out of the cabinet and onto the ground.

"It's Tom Kadow," someone shouted.

"Who's that?" Becka asked.

"He's a key grip . . . over the rigging crew."

Jaimie explained in a shaken voice, "He disappeared the first week of shooting, before you came. We thought he just couldn't take the country and quit. Everybody who knew him said he'd never walk off a set, but he didn't have any family to contact, so we never knew. . . ."

"He didn't walk off the set," Ryan said. "He must've been in that cabinet."

"Please," Jaimie said, "I think I'm going to be sick."

"C'mon, Jaimie." Ryan took her arm. "I'll walk you back to your trailer." As he passed Becka he added, "Guess this blows Z's theory to smithereens."

"What do you mean?"

"Now we've got ourselves a real victim."

Becka nodded slowly, her eyes still riveted to the corpse.

She did not follow Jaimie and Ryan but waited with the others as the doctor arrived to examine the body. Everyone appeared fairly shaken. Everyone but Dirk Fallon.

"Listen, Doctor," the director said. "I know examining the body and so forth can take a while. Would you like me to have someone help you move it to the medical tent or—"

"Disturbing the body might obscure something vital to my examination," the doctor replied.

Fallon nodded impatiently. "Well, I should think the cause of death is somewhat obvious. . . . The man doesn't have a drop of blood in him."

"That will be up to the officials at the morgue to decide. But it does bring up a curious problem, Mr. Fallon."

"What's that, Doctor?"

"Where's the blood? It's not in the cabinet, it's not on the floor, and it's not in the man."

"If you're asking me if I want to go on record suggesting that a vampire did this, the answer is no, Doc. But then, that is the only explanation, isn't it?"

"I don't have another at this time," the doctor said.

"Then can we get it out of here and go back to making our movie?"

Once again the doctor appeared shocked at the director's lack of compassion. "Mr. Fallon, a man has been murdered."

"And the only way I can stop there being more murders is to get this film finished as fast as I can and get us all out of here," Fallon said.

The doctor obviously did not approve of Fallon's attitude, but he agreed to move the body while he waited for somebody from the morgue to pick it up.

Minutes later, Becka watched as they hauled the body away. She felt a cold, numb knot in the pit of her stomach. In all of her encounters, no one had ever been murdered.

Until now.

"Enjoying your visit with us, Rebecca?" Dirk Fallon said as he walked past her without waiting for a response.

By now the crowd had started to break up, preparing for the next shoot. Since it was getting late, and since she really didn't want to be out here in the dark, Becka decided to go back to the hotel. It would have been nice to have some company, but Ryan obviously had other obligations.

Once again, she thought of Z's suggestion to love Jaimie with God's love. But seeing that corpse and realizing how wrong he'd been about vampires . . . well, couldn't he be just as wrong about handling Jaimie?

Then again, Z had never been wrong about anything before.

She wasn't sure if it was her fear of walking home alone or her concern for Jaimie. Maybe it was both. In any case, she decided to swing by Jaimie's trailer to see how she was doing. Besides, maybe Ryan would be ready to go back with her.

Becka navigated her way through the production trailers toward Jaimie's. She was about halfway there when, off in the shadows, she thought she saw movement.

She slowed to a stop and peered into the darkness.

There it was again. A black form moving through the shadows behind the trailers. A black form that looked a lot like a black billowing cape. A black billowing cape that she recognized all too well.

Becka went cold. It was the vampire.

Quickly she ducked for cover behind a truck. Then, ever so slowly, she peeked around the corner.

He was moving away, heading into the darkness.

Becka's first impulse was to scream, to shout out an alarm, to run in the opposite direction. But she knew that that would accomplish nothing. The vampire would simply disappear again and prepare to kill another.

Then, suddenly, a thought struck her. This was a golden opportunity. If she followed the vampire and found out where it lived, maybe they could come back in the daylight when it was asleep and destroy it. After all, vampires were supposed to be powerless in the day.

At least that's what all the legends said.

A wave of fear shuddered through Becka at the thought. Follow him? Was she insane? With a vampire's keen senses, there was a good chance he would spot her. And an even better chance that she would lose sight of him in the darkness.

Then again, when would an opportunity like this recur?

She took a deep breath to try to clear her mind.

"Dear God," she whispered, "I'm really scared. But I know you sent us over here to help Jaimie. I'm not sure what to do now, but you promised to protect us, and you've never let us down before. So . . . well, please, just be with me. Oh, and God, I'd sure appreciate it if you wouldn't let me get killed."

With the hesitant prayer—and with just a fraction more confidence—Becka moved away from the trailer and started following the creature.

The dark form moved effortlessly past the remaining trailers and into the nearby village. Becka did her best to keep him in sight. Maintaining a safe distance, she followed him down one, two, three alleys before he made a turn and headed to the edge of the town and out into a nearby field.

Becka nearly quit her pursuit at that point. After all, to hide behind trailers or alley walls was one thing; to be seen out in an open field with no cover was quite another.

But, remembering her prayer and the helpless look of fear she'd seen so often on

Jaimie's face, Becka pushed forward. She was no longer doing this for herself. She was doing this for Jaimie. That's what God had wanted. And if that's what God wanted, she'd rely on him for protection.

She moved from the cover of the wall and headed out into the field. Fortunately, there was a full moon and she could see the vampire's shadow, which allowed her to stay back a little bit farther.

He cut toward the right and began moving much faster. Faster than she could keep up.

She began losing ground.

Off in the distance, in the moonlight, she saw some kind of an iron fence. She thought the shadowy form had gone inside, but she was too far away to be sure.

A horrible thought struck. What if he decided to turn into a bat? No way could she keep up with him then. Or worse yet, what if he flew back and spotted her out here in the field? All alone, without any protection.

"I am with you always."

The verse Z had quoted rang in her mind, and she felt a little more peace. Why was she so afraid? She had the best protection anybody could have. And yet . . .

Beyond the large iron fence were what looked like short, tiny pillars. She caught a glimpse of the vampire's form moving past those pillars. But, as she squinted into the darkness, she realized that he wasn't moving past pillars. He was moving past tombstones.

He had entered a graveyard.

Surprisingly, the graveyard didn't frighten her. Maybe it was the prayer; maybe it was past experience. In any case, she was not afraid of the dead for the simple reason that she knew they were not there . . . just their bodies. And fearing dead bodies was like fearing somebody's old discarded shoes. Nobody was in them. Not anymore. People had used them once, but now they were left behind.

All she'd have to do was wait until daylight and then show up with some wooden stakes to drive through his heart, just like in the movies.

Revulsion shuddered through Becka. What was she thinking? She could never drive a stake through—

A low rumbling interrupted her thoughts. It wasn't loud enough to be thunder, and there was a scraping to it. Instantly she knew the sound—the rubbing of stone against stone. It could only mean one thing. The vampire was going back inside his crypt. If she didn't see where that crypt was now, she would never be able to find him.

She raced across the field toward the cemetery. Once she entered through the black iron gate, she slowed to a walk. The grave-yard was old, and many of the tombstones were in disrepair. Some had cracked and broken, with the split halves still lying on the ground. Others had crumbled into piles of rock.

As she moved past, she caught glimpses of dates: 1845 . . . 1811 . . . 1802.

She strained her ears to listen. Though she could no longer hear the scraping sound, she reasoned that if she had heard him open-ing his crypt, she would hear the same grat-ing rumble when he climbed inside and closed it.

She spotted another gravestone. A. J. Horn, 1723–1768. That was before America's independence!

Suddenly, Becka heard the rumbling and scraping again. It was just as she thought but far closer than she had imagined. She turned in the direction of the sound and silently moved through the grass. She moved by rows of tombstones as she peered intently at the larger crypts for any sign of movement.

Then, out of the corner of her eye, less than ten feet to her right, she saw it. A tall caped figure standing next to a crypt with an open lid.

It was him!

Startled and a little off balance, Becka's foot caught a broken piece of stone. She tried to catch herself but continued falling forward . . . headfirst . . . directly toward the caped figure and his open crypt.

She hit the ground and quickly rolled over, expecting to see the vampire looming above her, swooping down to sink his fangs into her neck.

But he was gone.

She scrambled to her feet. What was going on? Why hadn't he attacked? Surely he had seen her.

She spun around to the open crypt. The stone top was still ajar!

He was inside; she was certain of it!

A small part of Becka wanted to peer into that open crypt, but a greater part of her wanted to live. She didn't know why the vampire hadn't attacked, but she didn't want to stick around to give him a second chance.

She turned and sprinted out of the graveyard. She didn't stop until she saw the hotel.

～

When she arrived at the hotel, Becka found Ryan waiting for her in the lobby.

"So where'd you go?" he asked. "I came back to the set, and you were—"

The look on Becka's face stopped him cold.

"You've seen him!" Ryan said.

As they headed back into the hotel suite, Becka filled Ryan in on the details of tracking the vampire back to the cemetery. She also voiced her puzzlement over the thing not attacking her when she fell toward his open crypt.

"You know which grave is his?" Ryan asked.

Becka nodded.

"Then let's head out for the cemetery at dawn with a backpack full of sharp wooden stakes and some strong hammers."

"I don't know if I'm up to that," Becka said, her voice still a little high and unsteady. "Wait—what's that sound?"

They both froze. For the first time they noticed a soft beeping coming from the bedroom.

Becka took a deep breath. "It's just my computer. I left it on in case Z wrote back."

The two looked at each other and then, like lightning, raced into the room. Becka landed behind the computer, her hands already flying over the keyboard. A moment later she pulled up the message. It contained only nine words:

"God has not given us a spirit of fear." Z

"Is that it?" Ryan asked. "Is he still on-line?"

Becka shook her head. "No. But that's what he's been telling us ever since we got here. And this time, this time I think I've got an idea of what he means." Ryan looked at her, and she explained. "I've been letting fear cloud my thinking . . . and divide us. Jaimie and me, you and me, even Mom and me."

"And . . . ?" Ryan asked, not fully understanding.

"Don't you get it?" Becka asked. "Fear divides and builds more fear. But God has given us his power and his love—and the ability to think clearly."

"But Z doesn't even believe in the vampire," Ryan said.

Rebecca nodded. "All I know is that this whole time we've acted like we're in some kind of horror movie. But when I tracked that thing to the graveyard and when I prayed, it was like my fear started to go away. Because, at least for those few minutes, I knew God loved me and wouldn't let anything happen. And just as important, I knew I was doing it for Jaimie, out of *his* love for Jaimie."

Ryan continued to look at her.

"Then when I fell next to his crypt, I realized that my wits and knowledge of horror films and vampire trivia were *not* enough to save me. Only God could get me out of that tight spot. I still don't know what happened, why the thing didn't attack me, but I do know that we've been acting like we're trapped in a scary movie instead of thinking things through clearly. We're not using our minds, and we're certainly not using God's power."

Ryan nodded slowly. "I gotta admit, I really want to believe all that vampire stuff, 'cause it's kind of cool. But you're right; we sure haven't been fighting this thing like the other times."

Becka shook her head. "Wooden stakes, holy water, crucifixes—they're not exactly the tools we've used in the past."

Ryan flushed. "You're right. I guess it was easier to rely on them than on God." He sighed. "Maybe we should do some more praying."

Becka flashed him a grateful smile. "That's exactly what I was thinking."

Then without a word, Ryan reached out to take her hand, and they closed their eyes.

Finally, Becka began. "Lord, first of all, forgive me for all the resentment I've been feeling . . . and all the anger toward Jaimie and Ryan. Give me a love for Jaimie, *your* love, and please forgive us all for trying to solve this thing our way. Give us clear minds,

Lord. Help us to see your will and not allow ourselves to be so easily frightened and divided."

Ryan picked up where she left off. "And, God, help us to separate ourselves from all the craziness going on here. To do things and see things your way, instead of the way everybody else does."

As the two continued praying, Becka slowly felt a haze being lifted like a fog being blown away as she began to more clearly understand what was happening. And, as the fog lifted, a plan began to form.

ᴎ

Thirty minutes later, they were back at the computer carefully reviewing Z's old messages. Again and again, he had made it clear that vampires did not exist.

There are no such things as vampires. . . .
Look for another explanation.

And then there were his comments about fear. First the Bible verse he kept repeating: "God has not given us a spirit of fear." Becka knew it was true. When God's love and power were present, the fear was gone.

Ryan pointed at the screen, and Becka read:

The only true power this enemy has is the power
of fear. . . . Occult activity—whether real,
imagined, or counterfeit—is always based on fear.

And finally:

In every case, it becomes a matter of choice
to either trust in God's power and
experience his love or to believe in the
enemy's power and live in his fear.

Now, at last, she understood. It all came
down to faith. They could either believe the
stuff they saw and heard all around them or
they could believe in God. And his truth.
Becka slowly shook her head in wonder, mus-
ing over the mistakes she now saw they'd
made.

A moment later she grabbed a pencil and
paper. Ryan moved over to watch her write;
then he nodded. He pulled up a chair, and
together they worked out another plan. But
this one was different. It was based on God's
truth. It was based on his love—and the fact
that there are no such things as vampires.

9

First thing in the morning, Rebecca put the plan into action. Before she could really call upon the power of God, she had to start obeying his rules. And one of his first rules was that she had to make things right with those she had offended.

"Mom, can I talk to you for a moment?" she asked.

Mom sat at the small desk in their hotel room writing postcards. "Sure, honey."

Becka pulled up a chair across from her. "First of all, I'm sorry about the way I've been behaving. I mean, with John and all."

"That's all right, sweetheart."

"No, it isn't. I have no right to tell you what to do. I've been acting like I was your mother instead of the other way around and—"

"Listen, honey," Mom cut in. "It's really all right. John and I were never anything but acquaintances—"

Becka held up her hand. "No, Mom, seriously, if you want to see him . . ."

Mom smiled. "Becka, I don't want to see him."

Becka looked confused. "You don't?"

Mom shook her head. "I tried to tell you that, remember? As you pointed out, John isn't a Christian. So there really couldn't be anything between us but friendship. And he wasn't really even looking for that."

"He wasn't?"

Mom shrugged. "All he wanted was to spend some time with someone to keep from being bored." She smiled. "So you see? You really didn't need to worry, hon."

Becka sighed. "I guess I've just been feeling like everyone was against me from the first day we got here."

"It's been difficult for all of us."

"Well, if things work out the way I hope, we'll be going home very soon."

"Why's that?" Mom asked.

Becka smiled. "Because this time we're going to do it another way. This time we're going to catch a vampire God's way."

~

A few minutes later, Becka and Ryan got to work.

First, Ryan met with Tim and told him about Becka tracking the vampire to his crypt the night before. "We're planning on going back while it's daylight and catching him there. Will you help us?" Technically, it was the truth. They just weren't ready to tell Tim everything. Not yet.

"Of course I will," Tim replied. "But I've got a big conference call with money people this morning. I can't cancel it. After that I need to be on the castle set for a while. How does five o'clock sound?"

Ryan frowned. "That's quite a bit later than we were thinking. It gets dark around seven."

"That still gives us two hours," Tim said. "Unless you want to wait until tomorrow?"

Ryan shook his head. "No, he could move his coffin tonight. He knows we know where it is. Five o'clock will have to do."

Jaimie didn't arrive on the set until noon. The poor girl obviously needed all the rest she could get. When Becka finally found her, she was in the wardrobe truck trying on costumes.

"Hello, Becka," Jaimie said, looking at her in the mirror. "I'm not sure where Ryan is."

Becka smiled. "I was looking for you."

Jaimie tensed slightly. She obviously expected trouble. "All right . . ."

"No, it's nothing bad," Becka said. "Of course, I can't blame you if you're a little gun-shy around me. I have gone off on you a couple of times."

Jaimie said nothing, making it clear that she agreed with Becka.

"Anyway, I just came to say I'm sorry."

Jaimie raised an eyebrow in surprise. "You're sorry for going off on me?"

"Yeah. And I'm sorry for other things, too. Sorry I couldn't be more understanding, especially after all you've gone through. And . . . well . . . I'm sorry I was jealous about you and Ryan."

Jaimie looked at her quizzically. "Is this some kind of—"

"No, it's no trick," Becka said.

Jaimie continued to look at her. "All right, Becka," she said cautiously. "I'll accept your apology. As long as you understand that Ryan and I are . . . well, we're just friends."

"Oh . . . ," Becka said, not entirely believing her. "Well, that's between you and Ryan."

"Not that I didn't try," Jaimie said with almost a twinkle in her eye. "I mean, he is one of the cutest guys I've seen . . . but, well, last night he made it clear he has his eyes on somebody else."

"He did?" Becka's heart sank. As far as she had known, Jaimie was her only competition. Apparently there was somebody else. "Did he—" she cleared her throat—"tell you who?"

Jaimie broke out laughing. "It's you, Becka."

Becka caught her breath. And then once again she felt that old familiar warmth spread through her chest. She really did love him; there was no getting around it.

"Hey, guys."

She turned to see Ryan approaching. He shook his head, clearly displeased.

"I just talked to Tim on the phone," he said. "He's going to be delayed in town. He can't meet us until at least six o'clock."

"Six o'clock!" Becka protested. "That doesn't give us much time to get there and—"

The look on Ryan's face brought her to a stop. "There's more. The weather report says a big storm's coming in. It's going to get darker even earlier."

"Meaning . . ."

"Meaning we may have to confront the thing in the dark."

Becka took a deep breath and slowly let it out.

~

The scene that afternoon was to be filmed at Castle of the Arges, an ancient structure just a few miles outside of town. Though much of it was in ruins, people believed it was the actual castle used by Vlad the Impaler, the brutal overlord whose cruelty inspired the earliest vampire tales.

As Ryan and Becka rode to the location in one of the production shuttle vans, they couldn't help appreciating the irony. Here they were, about to watch a scene in which Dr. Van Helsing would drive a stake through the heart of the vampire—all the while wondering what their own vampire confrontation would be like just a few hours later.

When they arrived at the castle, they first looked for Tim, but he was nowhere to be found.

"He called my cell phone," Steve Delton said. "Left a message for you. Said he'd meet you at the hotel around six-thirty."

Becka and Ryan looked at each other with alarm. By six-thirty the sun would nearly be down.

"Thank you," Becka said. "If he calls again, tell him we'll be there."

More worried than ever, Becka and Ryan watched the filming in silence.

In the scene, Van Helsing had worked his way down to the cellar of the great castle in an effort to find the vampire's coffin. The room was large and cavernous, full of shadows and a musty smell.

The director called, "Action!" and Van Helsing lit his torch. At first he pretended to be excited over seeing the coffin, but as he approached it, he saw another coffin. Then another and another.

The room was filled with coffins.

Thinking back on the episode in the warehouse, Becka couldn't help whispering, "I know what that's like."

In desperation, Van Helsing ran from one coffin to the other, tipping several over, finding only dried bones.

"Cut!" Dirk Fallon's voice echoed loudly in the great room. "Print that. Excellent. Now we insert a shot of the light fading from the window and pick up with Van Helsing realizing he doesn't have any more time."

"That sounds pretty familiar, too," Ryan sighed.

Three crew members rushed out onto the set carrying a large mattress, which they positioned just out of camera range on the floor. Meanwhile, Steve Delton took his position on the set.

"OK!" Fallon shouted. "Ready, still rolling . . . and . . . action!"

Steve Delton again became Van Helsing. He stared out a window, a look of horror in his eyes. "The sun!" he cried. "It's going down!"

Then, with renewed frenzy, he charged into more coffins, tipping them over as fast as he could until . . .

"Looking for me, Doctor?"

Van Helsing looked up in terror at the chilling sound of the vampire's voice.

"Well," the vampire continued, "it's not very sociable to come to a man's home and make such a mess."

The doctor glared at him. "You're not a man, and this is not a man's home. . . . It's the lair of . . . a monster."

With that, the vampire exploded into fury, racing across the room, grabbing Van Helsing, and flinging him backward.

Even though Becka could see that the actor, Steve Delton, landed safely on the mattress that had been laid down, the powerful scene gave her chills.

"Cut!" Fallon yelled. "Good job, Steve. Print that. Now set up the reverse angle."

The same crew members hauled away the mattress and brought out a small rubber trampoline and some breakaway furniture— a couple of chairs and a coffee table.

Ryan glanced at his watch. Obviously he was getting nervous.

The crew set up the breakaway furniture, and the camera turned in the opposite direction to face the scene. A stuntman, dressed exactly like Steve Delton, came out and jumped up and down on the small trampoline, testing it a few times.

When all was ready, Fallon shouted, "Roll film . . . and . . . action!"

The stuntman bounced off the trampoline and smashed into the breakaway furniture.

Becka watched a nearby TV monitor, impressed that it looked exactly as if Van Helsing were thrown through the air and crashed into the furniture.

"Cut!" Fallon said. "We have to go again. Try to come off the tramp a little lower. It'll make for a better angle."

Ryan looked at his watch again. He turned to Becka. "It's four-fifteen. We can't wait for Tim any longer."

"All right," Becka said, fighting back the tension growing in her own body. "We'd better head out, then."

Ryan took a deep breath and nodded.

As they took the shuttle van back to the hotel, Becka spoke up. "Ryan, I want to apologize for the way I've been acting. We came here to help Jaimie, and I'm afraid I haven't been very supportive of that. I'm ashamed to say that the reason is . . . I was jealous."

"Jealous?" Ryan responded. "Of who? Me? I know I got to do some extra things, being on the crew and all, but it really wasn't that big of a—"

"Not you," Becka cut him off. "I wasn't jealous of you for working in the film. I was jealous of Jaimie being around you all the time."

"Oh," Ryan said, as a somewhat surprised expression lit his face.

Rebecca turned and sighed. *Men!* she thought. Their minds worked so differently from girls' that it was a wonder they worked at all!

"Actually," Ryan said, "I'm the one who should be apologizing to you."

Becka waited, hoping he wasn't about to tell her that he'd fallen for Jaimie.

"I should have been more understanding about how you were feeling," he said. "I just thought you were acting silly, but I never really tried to figure out why. That's not the way a friend should be. . . . I'm sorry."

Those few words touched Becka so deeply that she had to fight back a tightness in her throat. Just when she had been sure that Ryan was the most insensitive person in the world, he suddenly seemed to care about and understand her deepest feelings.

He looked at her, puzzled. "You OK?"

"I'm OK," she said hoarsely. "Thanks for asking."

The shuttle stopped in front of the hotel, and Becka and Ryan went in. They saw John Barberini then, and Becka added another element to their plan.

~

"You want me to *what?*" Barberini asked, looking at Becka suspiciously.

"Go with us to the cemetery. And bring your tape recorder and camera."

Barberini looked at her. Ever since Becka had doused him with the water, he had never seemed too comfortable around her. "You know where the vampire is buried?"

"Yes," she replied. "We're supposed to meet Tim Paxton at six-thirty to go over there."

"But it's barely five o'clock," Barberini said.

"That's part of our plan."

"I don't understand."

"I'll give you the whole scoop if you'll help us out."

Barberini hesitated for a moment and then reached over and picked up his camera bag. "Let's go," he said. "Oh, one more thing. Once we get into that cemetery, how do you know we're going to make it back out? I mean, without turning into zombies or something."

Ryan shrugged. "We don't."

Barberini nodded. "That's what I was afraid of."

Even at five o'clock in the afternoon, the old cemetery seemed eerie. Despite the remaining daylight, the approaching storm cast a spooky darkness over the area.

Becka, Ryan, and John Barberini crouched low behind some bushes next to the large crypt and waited.

"You sure you remember how to run that tape recorder?" Barberini asked.

Ryan glanced at the recorder in his hand. "No sweat."

Ten minutes later, Steve Delton hurried through the gate carrying an overnight bag. Tim Paxton trailed behind him. The wind of the storm whipped at their clothes.

"Hurry up, Tim!" Delton shouted over the wind. "We haven't got much time."

"I'm coming, I'm coming," Tim called. "It's your fault we're so late."

"It's Fallon's fault, not mine. Little creep wouldn't let me go until he made sure the fall matched. I mean, *I'm* the actor. The stuntman has to match *me*. They must've gone through a thousand dollars of break-away furniture."

"Who cares?" Tim said as he caught up to Delton. "With all the publicity this film is getting, we could triple the budget and still come out with a winner."

"Right," Delton agreed. "Just don't forget good old Van Helsing's bonus."

"You'll be well paid," Paxton said. "Now get ready."

In the bushes by the crypt, Rebecca and Ryan exchanged glances. This was the moment they'd been waiting for. Ryan clicked on the tape recorder, and they watched in silence as the two men continued to approach.

As he walked, Steve Delton opened his overnight bag and pulled out a latex mask. He stopped for a moment and carefully put it on.

In the bushes Ryan whispered, "You were right, Beck! He *is* the vampire."

John Barberini snapped a photo of Delton wearing the vampire mask. "How'd you figure this out?" he whispered.

"I realized that we'd all been reacting to

fear," Becka whispered. "So I tried doing what Z suggested and looked past the fear. If he was right and vampires don't exist, we had to ask ourselves who would benefit most by making something like this up. The only thing that benefited was the film. And then I realized that Tim, the film's producer, had been in on our plan to trap the vampire in the alley."

"So you set up this plan to capture Tim," Barberini said.

"What about Delton?" Ryan asked.

"I knew someone with the film had to be the vampire. At first I thought it was Fallon, but he's not tall enough. Then I remembered that, when Jaimie got burned by the crucifix, Delton was the one who put it around her neck. He probably put some kind of acid on the back of that cross. He was wearing gloves, so it didn't bother him."

"But what about the bat and the vampire floating outside your window?" Barberini asked.

"I don't know how they did those things," Becka said. "But since I've watched filming this week, I've learned that movie people can fake just about anything if they want to."

"Shhh . . . ," Ryan said. "They're coming this way."

"You straight on the plan?" Tim Paxton

asked as he and Delton finally came to a stop at the crypt.

"Got it," Delton said as he smoothed the mask onto his face. He reached back into his bag, pulled out a bottle of makeup, and began to carefully cover the edges.

"OK, then you won't mind running it by me," Tim prodded.

Delton sighed. "You and the kids get here about six-thirty. I'm lying in the casket, just like they expect. They lead you here to the crypt. You slide the stone cover over and open the casket. I open my eyes and grab your throat."

"Yeah," Tim agreed. "I'll insist on being the stake driver, and I'll keep the kids back, so I'll be leaning over to make it easy for you."

"OK," Delton said as he began attaching some long and pointed fingernails.

"Just be careful with those nails, all right?"

Delton nodded. "I've been doing this for a couple of weeks. I know what I'm doing."

Tim checked his watch. "I'll have to leave pretty soon. OK, what about the rest of it?"

Delton shrugged. "I grab your throat. The girl comes at me with the crucifix—"

"It could be the boy," Tim interrupted. "They'll both have them."

"OK, whoever comes at me with the cross,

I shove you back and then leap out of the grave and run away," Delton said.

"Yeah," Tim corrected, "but not right away. You have to kind of snarl and claw at them a couple of times before you run."

"Of course," Delton replied. "The standard routine."

"All right, then," Tim concluded. "I guess that's about it."

In the bushes by the large crypt, Becka looked at Ryan. He smiled and pointed to the running tape recorder.

Suddenly, to their surprise, John Barberini stood up, revealing himself and their hiding place. "No, that's not quite it, Tim."

The producer and the actor spun around, clearly surprised as Barberini continued. "It seems you weren't quite careful enough. Looks like your plan has been figured out."

Becka couldn't believe what Barberini was doing. They had agreed to hide and get everything on tape, not jump out and confront them.

"Be careful, John," Becka said as she rose to his side. But suddenly she was looking down the barrel of a .38 caliber revolver.

"I think *you're* the one who should be careful," Barberini replied as he held his gun on her.

Becka threw a panicked look to Ryan.

Barberini was in on the vampire hoax with Tim and Delton! They'd made a terrible mistake.

Maybe even a fatal one.

It started to rain. Big fat drops fell all around them.

"What happened, John?" Tim asked.

"She figured out it was a scam," Barberini said. "Didn't you, bright stuff?"

Becka swallowed and said nothing. The wind blew as rain continued to fall, soaking her hair, dripping down the side of her face.

Without warning, Barberini reached over and smacked her hard across the cheek. Ryan bounded to his feet in her defense, but he froze when Barberini swung the gun in his direction. Turning back to Becka, the reporter grinned. "I've been wanting to do that ever since you doused me with that holy water."

Becka held her cheek. Her face throbbed, and she could feel a welt already rising on the skin.

"You all right?" Ryan asked.

She wiped the rain from her face and nodded.

Ryan turned back to Barberini, furious. But Barberini's revolver kept him in check. "The only thing you kids didn't figure out was the bat at the Dominski warehouse."

Tim sighed. Ryan and Becka turned to him. The rain had plastered down his hair, and the wind blew his coat. He looked the most distressed of the three men. "There was a door just across the alley," he explained. "I made sure it was unlocked so Steve could make his getaway."

"Yeah," Delton said. "But not before leaving me something just inside the door. A large cage holding a nice big bat."

"What about the vampire outside my window?" Becka asked, pulling the wet hair from her face. "It looked so real."

"It *was* real," Delton answered. "My room is one floor up from yours. A little rigging, a little wire, and presto! Easy trick."

"Enough gabbing," Barberini insisted. "What do we do with them?"

Delton shrugged. "More victims for the vampire, I think."

Tim seemed reluctant. "Now wait a minute. Kadow's death was an accident. This would be . . . murder."

"An accident?" Ryan exclaimed.

Tim nodded. "That's how all of this started in the first place. Steve, Kadow, and I were looking over the mansion location. We were trying to decide if we needed to run some extra rigging to have the vampire swoop away at the end of the party scene. Kadow was up in the rafters trying to show me how he'd stage it when he slipped and fell. He hit the back of his head on one of the stones." Tim shook his head. "He died instantly.

"Kadow didn't have any family or anyone who cared what happened to him. When he was killed, we realized we could capitalize on his death. So we started a few rumors about a real vampire and came up with our whole scheme to scare Jaimie—and before anyone could accuse us of a hoax, we had Kadow's body turn up, drained of blood."

"That was messy," Delton added, the rain streaming down his stringy hair and into his face. He grinned at Becka and Ryan. "'Course, now that I've got the hang of it, I shouldn't have any trouble doing it again."

"Stop it, Steve." Tim began pacing, obviously upset. "Up to now we've just been guilty of a scam, but killing innocent kids is another thing entirely."

"I'm not going to jail again," Barberini growled. "When you guys brought me in on this plan to get publicity, I agreed. But I've done time in the pen. I'm not going back there again. I'd kill these kids first. I'd kill both of you, too, if I had to."

Becka closed her eyes. Her instincts about John Barberini had been right all along.

"All right," Delton agreed. "But don't

shoot them, for crying out loud. Vampires don't shoot people. Let's use the fangs we used on Kadow's neck." He reached into his overnight bag and pulled out a set of steel fangs. "They don't look so pretty, and you have to plunge them in hard with your hands, but they do the job, and they leave good marks."

Ryan and Becka exchanged terrified looks. *God, help us!* Becka prayed. From the look on Ryan's face, she was sure he was praying, too.

"You first," Barberini ordered Becka.

"Take her over by the crypt," Steve said. "It'll look better."

Barberini motioned with his gun for Becka to move to the crypt. She looked at Ryan one more time before Barberini gave her a push, and she did as she was told.

Delton pulled on a pair of black leather gloves. Then, crossing to Becka, and with Barberini holding a gun to her back, he brought the steel fangs up to her throat.

"Wait!" Tim shouted over the wind. "There must be another way!"

"There's no other way," Barberini yelled.

"He's right, Tim," Delton agreed. "It'll all be over in a minute."

Both Barberini and Delton focused their attention on Becka as Tim turned around, not wanting to see the killing.

Delton leaned in close to Becka, looking for the artery in her neck. Even in the pouring rain she could feel his hot breath against her skin.

Suddenly Ryan made his move. With all of his might he lunged at Barberini's arm. He hit him hard, sending the man slipping and staggering as the gun flew out of his hand. With a roar of anger, Delton reached for Ryan—who managed to spin around and land a good right hook, breaking the man's nose.

"*Augh!*" Delton cried, grabbing his nose. He looked at his hand and saw the blood. Furious, he lunged for Ryan.

Forgotten by her captors for the moment, Becka spotted the gun in the mud and leaped for it. But she wasn't quick enough.

Barberini slammed into her, knocking her aside, and scooped up the wet pistol. "That's enough!" he shouted.

Ryan and Delton stopped grappling.

Delton reached for the steel fangs again. "I'm killing the punk first!" He sneered as he angrily swiped at the blood streaming from his nose. "And believe me—" he leaned forward, practically spitting into Ryan's face— "it's *not* going to be painless!"

"Stop talking about it and do it!" Barberini shouted.

Becka prayed with all of her might as Delton, grinning maniacally, lifted the fangs up to Ryan's throat. And then, just as he was pressing them against the vein: "Hold it right there!" A voice rang out from nowhere.

Delton spun around.

"Drop the gun," another voice shouted.

"You're outnumbered and outgunned," came a third.

Becka watched as three uniformed police officers approached, followed closely by Mom and Jaimie.

"I said, drop the gun!" the first policeman shouted, leveling his own weapon at Barberini, who let his pistol fall and raised his hands.

"Mom!" Becka ran to her mother.

"It's a good thing Jaimie told me where you were," Mom said.

"I got a message from Z," Jaimie said. "He said you might be in danger."

Becka and Ryan looked at each other in amazement. For once they didn't care how Z always knew what was happening. They were just very, very glad he did.

10

By noon the next day, the weather had cleared, and Rebecca, Ryan, and Mom were leaving for the airport. Jaimie was to stay on another week to finish the film. The doctor's report verified that Tom Kadow had died from a blow to the head. Since both Tim Paxton and Steve Delton were being held in jail pending their trial for fraud, the studio had sent someone else out to supervise production. The stunt double would film Van Helsing's last scene.

Steve Delton was also being charged with attempted murder, as was John Barberini.

"I'm going to miss you guys an awful lot," Jaimie said in the lobby while they waited for a production shuttle van to take them to the airport. "It won't be the same without you."

"You'll be done and out of here before you know it," Ryan replied.

"And don't forget to call us when you get home," Becka added.

"Yeah, if you ever come to visit, we'll throw a big party in your honor," Ryan said.

"Just don't make it a Halloween party," Jaimie joked. "I've had enough of that stuff for a while."

The shuttle pulled up outside and honked its horn. The group headed out the door and toward the curb.

"Well," Jaimie said as they arrived and the driver loaded their luggage, "you two take care."

Becka and Ryan nodded.

Jaimie reached up and gave Ryan a friendly peck on the cheek. "For luck." She smiled.

Becka could see Ryan's face reddening as Jaimie turned to her. "You've got a good thing there, Rebecca Williams. Don't lose him."

Becka was unsure how to respond. Fortunately, she didn't have to. Almost immediately, Ryan was reaching out and taking her hand. "She doesn't intend to," he said, looking at Becka and smiling. "And neither do I."

Becka returned the smile, once again feeling those little flutters deep inside her stomach.

After another set of good-byes, they turned to climb on board the van. Once inside, they looked out the window and waved one last time to Jaimie as the vehicle pulled away from the curb and started for the airport.

As they headed down the road, Becka again felt Ryan take her hand. And, as she looked into his deep blue eyes, she completely forgot anything and everything about Jaimie Baylor.

"I tell you," Ryan sighed as he settled back into his seat, "between being in a foreign country, working on a movie, and getting caught up in all this vampire stuff, I feel like we've had enough adventure to last us a long, long time."

"Me, too," Becka said. "I just want to get home to good old America. The most adventure I plan to have is relaxing, catching up on some magazines, and finally having a normal teenage life."

"I don't think there's any such thing as a normal teenage life, is there?" Mom teased from the seat behind them. "But even if there were, I'm afraid you're going to be disappointed."

Becka turned to look at her. "Disappointed? Why?"

Mom smiled and held out a piece of paper. Becka took it, then looked at her mother, eyes wide. "It's a telegram." She glanced at Ryan. "From Scotty."

Mom nodded. "The gentleman at the front desk gave it to me just as we were leaving."

"What's he say?" Ryan asked.

Becka read it out loud:

DEAR MOM.
RYAN'S MOTHER WILL PICK YOU
GUYS UP AT THE AIRPORT. I'LL
PROBABLY COME, TOO. CAN'T WAIT
TO HEAR WHAT HAPPENED AND TO
TELL YOU WHAT Z'S GOT PLANNED
NEXT.

"What?" Ryan exclaimed. "Z's got something else planned?"

"There's more." Becka returned to the telegram.

TELL BECKA AND RYAN THAT WE
GET TO GO TO L.A. WE'RE GOING

TO HANG OUT WITH SOME ROCK
AND ROLLERS. LOOKS LIKE WE GET
TO DUKE IT OUT WITH SOME
SORTA SATANIC BAND OR SOME-
THING. IS THAT COOL OR WHAT?

SEE YOU SOON.
SCOTT

Becka and Ryan looked at each other.
They each took a deep breath and slowly let
it out. So much for the peace and rest they
wanted. It didn't look like it would be coming their way anytime soon. Apparently
another battle waited to be fought. One for
which Z was already preparing them.

Becka settled back into the seat and leaned
her head on Ryan's shoulder. She was grateful to have him by her side. But she was even
more grateful to know that God was there,
that he would never leave her.

Especially with what was coming . . .

Especially when it seemed there was no
end to the ways, shapes, and sizes in which
darkness attacked . . .

AUTHOR'S NOTE

As I developed this series, I had two equal and opposing concerns. First, I didn't want the reader to be too frightened of the devil. Compared to Jesus Christ, Satan is a wimp. The two aren't even in the same league. Although the supernatural evil in these books is based on a certain amount of fact, it's important to understand the awesome protection Jesus Christ offers to all who have committed their lives to him.

This brings me to my second and somewhat opposing concern: Although the powers of darkness are nothing compared to the power of Jesus Christ and the authority he has given his followers, spiritual warfare is not something we casually stroll into. The situations in these novels are extreme to create suspense and drama. But if you should find yourself involved in something even vaguely similar, don't confront it alone. Find an older, more mature Christian (such as a parent, pastor, or youth leader) to talk to. Let them check the situation out to see what is happening, and ask them to help you deal with it.

Yes, we have the victory through Christ, but we should never send in inexperienced soldiers to fight the battle.

Oh, and one final note. When this series was conceived, there were really no bad guys on the Internet. Unfortunately that has changed. Today there are plenty of people out there trying to draw young folks into dangerous situations through it. Although the characters in this series trust Z, if you should run into a similar situation, be smart. Anyone can *sound* kind and understanding, but their intentions may be entirely different. All that to say, don't take candy from strangers you see . . . or trust those you don't.

Bill

FORBIDDEN ◘ DOORS

Want to learn more?

Visit Forbiddendoors.com on-line for
special features like:

- a really cool movie
- post your own reviews
- info on each story and its
  characters
- and much more!

Plus—Bill Myers answers your questions!
E-mail your questions to the author. Some
will get posted—all will be answered by
Bill Myers.